THE SNAKE'S CANYON CAPER

THE PIRATE QUEENS MYSTERY SERIES

RL DONOVAN

EDGE HOUSE PRESS

1

"Katrina, do you have a minute? Professor Frost?"

Fuck.

The dean.

She fought the urge to dive under her desk and stayed still.

Knock. Knock.

Katrina rose and swung open the door. "Dean Bullard. Please come in."

A round little man with cauliflower ears, nicknamed Mr. Potato-head by Katrina's colleague, trundled in and plopped down on a hard chair. He wiped his brow and leaned forward.

Katrina sat down and pasted on her how-can-I-serve-you-today-white-man face.

"I'm glad I caught you. We need to talk," Bullard said.

Hell.

"Shane Bivens has made an accusation."

"Of what?"

Shane Bivens, professor of philosophy, was capable of anything. But what had she done recently—other than existing?

"He says you tampered with the rank and tenure results for an assistant professor."

"With all due respect, that is a load of hogwash, if you'd like the polite term."

The dean leaned back in his seat and folded his hands behind his head.

Katrina mirrored his movement, sitting back and trying to relax. "Does he have any evidence?"

"He says you used affirmative action to promote Quincy Knight."

This was too much. Katrina thought back to last night. She hadn't left campus until 9:30 p.m., stuck in a departmental meeting about assessment loops. Before that it had been the technology committee. Dinner had been leftover cold vegetables, eaten at her desk. She still had to prep for her 3 p.m. lecture. And her inbox was stuffed with unanswered student emails. Underneath it all lay the letter dated three weeks ago, the one she'd put off forever: the builder saying her house needed a new roof before the winter set in. Right. On her salary.

She leaned in so close to the dean's face she could see the beads of sweat trembling on his forehead.

"Let me tell you something, *Dean Bullard*. Shane Bivens classifies all women as either 'fuckable' or 'unfuckable.' That's what he tells his male colleagues. He sleeps with his students and yells racial epithets I don't care to repeat. At a university supposedly dedicated to social justice. And since I'm friends with his administrative assistant, I suspect he embezzles what meager funds we have." She paused. "So do you trust him or me?"

She already knew the answer before she asked the damn question.

He rose and buttoned his too-tight blazer over his ample belly. "If you'd like to report these allegations to HR, they will follow an appropriate legal process. In the meantime, I suggest you prepare for a full-scale investigation."

———

Katrina slumped at her desk, contemplating physical revenge

scenarios. Zeynep popped her head, framed with a glossy dark brown bob, around the door frame. "Would you sign these checks? They should be sent today." She peered at Katrina. "Are you okay? I just saw the dean leave your office."

"Admit it, you want the dirt," Katrina said. "Have a seat. Want some chocolate?" She broke off a piece of Cadbury and handed it to her. "He thinks I did something I didn't do. Or I should say he cannot prove. Shane Bivens—of all people—accused me of being crooked. The nerve."

Zeynep giggled. Then chuckled. Then laughed. She wiped away rivulets of tears.

"Thanks, I can see I can count on you in a crisis."

"Oh, I'm sorry," she said, waving her hand as she took a deep breath. "It's so rich coming from Darth Vader. Bullard hasn't a clue about Bivens, does he?"

"But he's been here ten years! He should know better."

"You should be dean," whispered Zeynep.

"Oh no, not on your life. Not a chance. This university gets more ridiculous every year. I know it's not only this university, but it's the damn social justice mission hypocrisy which makes it unbearable."

"Tell me about it," said Zeynep. "They're planning to cut staff pay. Doreen's been visiting the food bank."

Katrina shook her head. When had she believed in higher education institutions? Ah, right, Katrina, she thought. Never. Not that she didn't believe in higher education in theory. It was in practice where it fell apart. Lately, the fear mentality that oozed in every corner of this institution had seeped into her bones. Five years ago she would never have considered hiding under her desk.

Zeynep studied her fingernails and glanced at the brass wall clock. The clock Katrina had set ten minutes ahead so students wouldn't linger in her office. "I'd better get going." She gripped the desk and lifted herself up.

"Why are you wincing?"

"Oh, it's nothing. Something in my back. I'm supposed to go to the doctor this week. I've been avoiding it, though, since my deductible is so high."

"Should the department buy something to help out at your desk?"

Zeynep shook her head and turned toward the door. Then her head snapped back.

"You know, Katrina, this university owes us a whole lot. I say it's payback time."

2

———

"What do you mean by payback?" Katrina asked.

But Zeynep had already been diverted by Professor Blankenship. She knew Zeynep disliked working with Blankenship, so Katrina didn't press further.

A small, lithe student in studious black glasses appeared at the door. Her hair made her look like she had stepped out of a volume conditioner commercial, though it was pulled back into a long swinging ponytail. "I'm Tala Guinto—we had an appointment at two?" she said tentatively.

Katrina shuffled mounds of paper on the desk. "Oh, yes. Please sit down."

"Thanks for taking time to discuss the paper."

"No problem. That's why I'm here. What questions do you have?"

Long experience with office hours had taught Katrina to sense whether a meeting was really about a student's paper—or about something else. This particular meeting was definitely about something else.

Tala slid a neat stack of papers onto Katrina's messy desk, making sure her papers avoided Katrina's own stacks spread across the desk. Setting her pen down, she folded her hands in her lap. "I wanted to talk to you about whether my thesis makes sense, but before we do …"

Uh-oh, here we go. Katrina stuck her foot on the desk, bracing for impact.

"I wanted to explain why I haven't been in class." She paused.

Was Katrina supposed to say something?

"My girlfriend, you see …"

Relationship trouble. Of course. A hazard of being a woman professor. Everyone came to her for therapy. Even when she tried to be an intimidating teacher, they still arrived in droves.

"Yes?" Katrina pulled out her obligatory box of Kleenex. This gesture always prompted tears to flow.

And flow they did. "My girlfriend left me, and my mom and dad have entered deportation proceedings," Tala said.

Oh Jesus. Katrina melted.

"Oh, I'm so sorry to hear that, Tala. Let's talk about your options for completion since we're already halfway through the semester."

"That's what makes it so hard!" Her Kleenex disappeared into her balled fist. "The registrar told me I can't take a hardship withdrawal."

"Why?"

"They won't give me a clear-cut answer. They said it's too late."

Katrina slammed her coffee cup down on the desk. Tala jumped.

"This goddamn fucking university is going to pay."

———

TALA LEFT in a cloud of confusion and tears. Katrina told her she'd be in touch.

A muffled ring came from her desk. Katrina dug through her papers till she saw a blinking red light on her ancient phone. Now what?

"Hello. This is Professor Katrina Frost."

"Hi, Katrina. It's Adi from Student Services. I'm sorry to call, but it's urgent."

Pulse rising, Katrina propped her tired head on one hand. "Go on. It's already been the day—or should I say month—from hell."

"We have a student who tried to commit suicide."

"I'll be right over." She paused. "But why me?"

"The student's friends asked for you to be present. When I asked why, they were vague. They said they trust you."

"Hmph. I wish they'd write about it on my teaching evaluations." Katrina shook her head. "Sorry. I'll join you in a few minutes."

Adi's voice lowered. "And Dean Hackett will join us."

"Oh, fantastic. This day is getting better and better."

"Thanks. I know it's a pain."

Katrina gulped and closed her eyes. Then she jolted upright, left her office and flew down the stairs, wanting to get away from her desk littered with problems as fast as possible.

Dead leaves bombarded her head in a gust of wind. Katrina blinked in the weak sunlight, just strong enough to make her wish she had her sunglasses. Classes were in session, so only a few stragglers galloped toward their class or moseyed home. As another gust of wind ruffled her hair, she popped up her collar against the chill. Her stomach clenched as the administration building came into view. Perhaps she could run away? Run home? She spun around as if to go and then spun back, gritting her teeth. If she put it off, the issue would only grow larger, as would her inbox.

"Excuse me, Professor Frost?" A small mouselike girl wearing tangerine lipstick approached, her brown clothes matching her brown hair.

"Ellie, good to see you. How are you?"

Her eyes darted around the quad. "I'm fine. I wanted to thank you for your museum internship recommendation. They accepted me!"

A warm glow of pride spread over Katrina. "Fantastic. I knew you'd get it."

"You're not like they say. You're not at all frosty," Ellie blurted out. She held a hand up to her mouth. "Sorry. My boyfriend says you're frosty. You're a hard grader."

Katrina sighed. "Does he? It's not the first time and certainly not the last. Maybe he'll change his mind, but if not, I really couldn't give a—"

"Professor Frost!" A hand patted her arm.

Ellie's eyes widened, as if seeing two professors greet each other in a friendly way was equivalent to watching some unknown cheetah mating ritual.

"Professor Scott!" Katrina rejoined. "I was telling Ellie here—"

But Ellie had scampered away.

Strange child, thought Katrina.

"You mean Ellie is a strange child?"

"Ah, sorry, Tamika. Did I say that out loud?" She surveyed Tamika Scott, professor of economics. Her friend's close-cropped hair didn't hide the circles under her normally smiling eyes. Her makeup had a caked-on quality, as if applied by one who is going through the motions.

Katrina grabbed her hand. "Are you alright?"

Her frown turned upward into a smile. "Yes—well, no. I just received a nasty email from a so-called colleague."

"What the hell? Is Mercury in retrograde or what? I can't handle any more bad news today."

Tamika's raspberry lips set in a grim line. "It's about to become worse. Are you coming to the meeting with Adi too?"

Katrina gave her a wry smile. "I should've known they'd call you in. They ask you to fix everything, don't they?"

"Yes. Though Dean Hackett is slick as an eel, I wasn't called in as a fixer this time." She pulled out a Kleenex and dabbed her eyes.

"Why, then?"

"The student who attempted suicide? He's my nephew. Gabriel Lomax."

3

———

A string of Christmas lights twinkled behind a tangle of ivy arranged neatly around the window.

"Have a seat. Associate Dean Hackett will arrive shortly." Adi held up a forefinger. The long undercut of red hair obscured Adi's face as their pink nails clacked against the keyboard.

Tamika and Katrina sat down in comfortable oversized chairs. A minute later, Tamika's diminutive body rocketed out of her chair.

Adi stopped clacking and looked up. "What's wrong? Did someone spill something on the chair?"

Hand to her cheek, Tamika's shocked face showed the beginnings of a smile. But Katrina could tell it wasn't genuine.

"I'm so sorry, Adi, but who was sitting in this chair before me?"

Adi leaned back in their chair and chewed on a pen. "Dean Bullard."

"That bean counter certainly is busy this morning," muttered Katrina. "He already visited me."

Ignoring Katrina, Adi said, "Why? Why does it matter?"

"You'll say I'm crazy," said Tamika. "But I sensed something nefarious sat in the chair before me."

"Nefarious is an excellent word for Dean Bullard," said Katrina.

"Don't laugh at me!"

"I'm not! Seriously. Is this a newly developed skill of yours? You're such a scientific economist."

"Don't listen to Katrina. Be yourself," said Adi.

Katrina snorted. "Perfect student development line, Adi."

The door swung open, but Associate Dean Edward Hackett did not enter. His height was only slightly diminished by him leaning against the doorknob. Katrina thought he must have been handsome in his youth, but years of hard drinking had changed him. His pasty white nose featured broken capillaries and his red-rimmed eyes were watery. And not watery with tears. Katrina figured he had never shed a tear in his life.

"Right," he said, oblivious to the scene he'd interrupted. "Let's get this over with."

The door closed with such force it sent ivy leaves and papers flying.

Dean Hackett plopped down in Tamika's former chair and smoothed his enormous salt-and-pepper mane. Tamika sat on a hard plastic chair in the corner. Katrina thought it looked like a time-out chair from preschool, but she knew Adi would never endorse such an outdated idea. Though Katrina often thought physical disciplining of some students would go a long way.

"So we're here about an attempted suicide," said Hackett flatly.

Tamika shot him a murderous glance.

Adi's face contorted in agony. They laced their fingers together and sighed. "Yes. And we've asked Professor Scott," said Adi, nodding at Tamika, "to be present as the student in question is her nephew."

Hackett looked over his shoulder at Tamika. Instead of moving his chair so she would be included in the circle, he said, "I'm so sorry." He whipped his head forward.

Tamika grabbed the seat of her chair and slid forward, right in between Katrina and Hackett. He shifted his shoulders uncomfortably.

"What happened? What are our next steps?" asked Hackett.

Adi pursed their lips. "A Swan Hall resident assistant found

Gabriel unconscious this morning after knocking on his door and receiving no answer. Gabriel is stable in the ER, thank God, but we don't know how he tried to take his life." Adi shuffled papers on the desk, coming up with a folded, worn note.

Katrina snatched the note before Hackett could grab it. She opened it and began to read: "'Dear Auntie T.'" She paused, eyes wide. "Is that you?"

Tamika shook her head. "No, Gabriel's parents died and he was raised by a cousin—he calls her Auntie T. I'm Auntie Ta." She stared at her knees.

Katrina continued. "'The stress is too much. I'm sorry, but I have to do this. I love you.'"

Rain splashed against the window and pattered on the roof.

The Christmas lights winked at Katrina.

"Gabriel's friends report he was under a lot of pressure. His chemistry professor never had a kind word for him. And his friends also suspect he was being bullied."

Hackett snorted. "Everyone throws that term around these days. What does it mean? The unfortunate fact is that college is stressful and isolating. Must be the case here, sadly."

Tamika's perfectly manicured fingernails dug into her bag but her face remained impassive.

Sensing it was her turn to talk—or rather seizing the opportunity—Katrina said, "I disagree. Based on what Gabriel's friends said, I think this calls for further investigation. If Adi leads the investigation, then I suggest interviewing the chemistry professor and Gabriel's friends further to find out more about these bullies."

"I agree." Adi leaned back in the captain's swivel chair.

Without waiting for Tamika's response, Hackett said, "We're under budgetary pressures, and while this is a sensitive issue, I think we can let it go. Especially since the student didn't die." He paused, pointing at Adi. "She said the boy is in stable condition."

The rhythm of the rain was broken by Dean Hackett's fingers drumming on his chair.

With narrowed eyes, Adi breathed, "I go by they/them, Dean

Hackett. And I suggest you not refer to Professor Scott's nephew as 'boy.'" Adi paused. "I suggest we bring in Assistant Dean Roberts, even though he's in the School of Education. He's had a great deal of experience dealing with these matters."

Hackett's face turned an unlovely blotchy red. He sputtered, "You're accusing me of being racist and, what would it be called? God knows. Un-PC, I suppose. I demand an apology."

Tamika stood up, sending her hard plastic chair flying backwards. She stood still, but Katrina observed her shaking hands. Her mouth opened, but nothing came out.

"Adi and Professor Scott, would you mind if I had a word alone with Dean Hackett?" Katrina turned to Adi and winked, out of the line of sight of Hackett.

Adi sprang up and guided Tamika out. Tamika slammed the door behind them.

Katrina rose from her seat and paced near the ivy-covered window.

Hackett walked to the door. "I can't imagine what we have to discuss. The matter is settled." He ran his fingers through his glorious mane.

"Sit down."

"What did you say?" Red spots reappeared on his cheeks.

"You heard me, I said sit down."

Katrina jammed her hand in her pocket and pulled out a black tourmaline worry stone. She clasped it in her palm so Hackett couldn't see it. The cool stone soon turned warm in her hot hands.

He snorted. "I don't take orders from you." He turned the door handle.

"I wouldn't do that if I were you," she said in a low voice. "Leila Vantu."

The door handle shook under Hackett's large hand. He groped for a chair and lowered himself down.

"Glad I have your attention. Amazing what one name will do."

"What do you want?"

"I want you to hand over this investigation to Dean Roberts, as

Adi suggested. You will do whatever Dean Roberts wants. Understood?"

With closed eyes, Hackett nodded. He rose to leave.

"And if you retaliate against Adi, I won't hesitate to mention Leila."

Silence.

"Understood?"

He nodded, back turned toward the door. He muttered in a half whisper, "Crazy fat bitch. I'll..."

"What did you say, Dean Hackett?" The words hurt, but Katrina was more satisfied with her supersensitive hearing than she was disappointed by his words.

"Nothing, Professor Frost."

With an extra touch of malice, Katrina said, "You are dismissed."

4

———

"Ah, that's better," sighed Katrina. She smacked her lips and held her mug aloft.

"Cheers." Tamika clinked her mug against Katrina's. The mug read, *The answer is no*. Tamika turned it around in her hands and laughed. "It's a good lesson for you and for me. As I get older, it's easier to say no, but the problem is there are more requests."

"Tell me about it." Katrina drained her mug, enjoying the fiery trail of scotch down her throat. "This is delicious. Dave Damsen gave it to me after I chewed out Dean Bullard in public."

"But you and Damsen aren't exactly allies, are you?"

"Well, no. But he has respect for anyone who stands up to Dean Bullard. Damsen's old school."

Tamika set down her mug and rested her head against the wall. "Thanks for the drink. I needed it after that scene."

"Hackett is a bastard. Always has been."

"I don't understand the administration at this school." Tamika stared at the ceiling. "My friends at other schools have problems, but the administration is at least more like the faculty—you know, people to watch out for, but also people who care." She sighed and took another sip of scotch. "Sometimes I fantasize about leaving…" She trailed off. "By the way, what did you tell Hackett?"

Katrina squared a stack of papers on her desk. "Oh, I had some information I wanted to share."

Tamika's face lit up. "You have dirt on him, don't you?" She slapped the desk. "I knew it. You always know what's going on."

"Well, maybe." Katrina shifted uncomfortably. She regularly passed by Hackett's office to get to one of the better copiers on campus. Over the past few weeks, she'd seen Leila in his office—during office hours—but had heard flirtatious laughs that immediately stopped when she passed by. Hackett had a reputation when it came to women students, and campus gossip was rarely wrong about this type of thing.

"But why wouldn't you use it against him in some way? Not to hurt him, but to stop his bad behavior?" asked Tamika.

"To tell you the truth, I had a lucky guess. That he was sleeping with—or at the very least, was in an inappropriate relationship with —a student."

"So? You hit the jackpot!"

"If I were to expose him, HR would investigate and they'd bring in the student. I know this student is in a precarious mental state already, so an investigation might put her over the edge. If I cover it up but use it as leverage against Hackett, I'm worried he might pressure the student or…do something worse. It's not worth it."

Tamika grinned. "Well, at least you were able to use it for a bit of vengeful satisfaction on my behalf. I appreciate it—beyond words. But you'd better watch your step."

"What's that noise?" asked Katrina.

Tamika leaned over. She popped back into view with a slip of paper in her hand.

"Here, let me read it." Katrina scanned the note. "It's from a student of mine, a computer science major. She says she has vital information and wants to meet tonight."

"About what?"

"She doesn't say. Should I go?"

"Depends on if you trust her."

"At the bottom, she says Zeynep will be there," said Katrina.

"What? Why would Zeynep be there?"

"It says Zeynep encouraged her to go to me."

"Is Zeynep here? Can we ask her?"

"No, she's gone home. I'll text her."

Before she hit send on her phone, an alarm rang.

The fire alarm.

———

"Excuse me." Shoulders hunched against the autumn chill, Katrina tapped a campus safety officer's elbow. "Is there really a fire? It's an odd time of day for a drill."

He sniffed and cracked his knuckles. "It's definitely not a drill. But someone might have accidentally pulled the alarm."

Tamika whispered to Katrina, "It can't have been an accident because it's hard to set off the alarm. Besides, I can tell."

"Is this your sixth sense again?"

"It's odd. Today was the first time I've ever felt it. And you know I don't believe in new-age nonsense. But it was so strong when I sat down in that chair. And then, just now, I had the same sense."

Katrina wiped mist from her eyes and shivered. "So why would someone deliberately set off the alarm?"

"Didn't you just threaten someone, sweetheart?"

Tamika was the only person who could get away with calling Katrina sweetheart.

"Yes, but they wouldn't do that, right?"

Tamika snorted. "You know as well as I do these people will stop at nothing to get what they want."

"Yes..." Katrina shivered. To distract herself, she scanned the faces in the crowd, lit up only by the streetlights. Then she spotted it—the new math professor's signature long tweed coat. Jeremy Jenkins. She sighed as he melted into the crowd and turned back toward her building. Pointing at her office window on the third floor, she whispered, "Look!"

"What is it? What do you see?"

"I turned off the lights after we left. Didn't you notice the light spinning around in my office? Someone's in there! Do you think it's Hackett?"

"C'mon! Let's find out—follow me." Tamika waved Katrina around the back of the building.

Katrina stood in place, blinking through her wet, droopy bangs.

Tamika backtracked. "What are you waiting for? Let's get the bastard!"

Arms crossed, Katrina peered again at her office window. The flashlight glow returned. "Alright. But only because the light is still on —I'm not sure about this plan."

"Well, what are we waiting for? To get soaked?" Tamika scampered across the stone pathway, holding her jacket above her head as protection against the raindrops.

Shaking her head, Katrina ran after her. She wrinkled her nose in the stairwell.

"Whew! This place smells like hot yoga. Like hot ass," said Tamika.

Katrina giggled. "Let's go." She put her hand on the light switch but then stopped. "Should we turn on the light?"

"Maybe not. I'll turn on my phone flashlight."

They wound their way up to the third floor. Katrina leaned her bulk against the fire door.

"Shit. It's stuck."

5

"Does it need a key?" Tamika jiggled the knob.

"No, it's supposed to be unlocked so people don't get stuck in the stairwell."

"Like us?" Tamika gave Katrina a weak grin.

"Could whoever's in the building have locked it themselves?"

"It's possible, but it seems unlikely. Wouldn't it be a perfect escape route?"

Tamika stood on tiptoe, barely able to peer out of the small window. Without her three-inch heels, she was a full head shorter than Katrina. "I saw a flash of light." She turned to Katrina. "Here. Let's try together. Ready? One, two, three!" They hurled their bodies against the door and tumbled into a heap in the hallway.

In the darkness, a light flashed again near her office door. Then it went out.

"They've seen us," breathed Katrina.

"I'm too old for this," whispered Tamika.

"It was your idea!"

"Too true." She rubbed her toes and inserted her burgundy heels into her bag. "Do we have a weapon—just in case?"

They rummaged in their bags. Tamika held up a tiny pair of sewing scissors. Katrina snorted and held her hand over her mouth.

"What? Have you got something better? These little scissors saved me from many tight spots."

"Sorry," hissed Katrina. She held up a thin metal-tipped Pilot pen.

Now it was Tamika's turn to snort. "And you had the nerve to make fun of me? We're definitely two badasses with tiny scissors and a pen." She crouched down, scissors in one hand, and moved stealthily in her stockinged feet toward Katrina's door.

With her back against the wall, Katrina listened. Heavy breathing came from inside her office, but there was no movement. The bastard must've heard them. It was risky, but if she threw something across the doorway in the opposite direction, it might be enough to make him bolt.

As if in sync with her thoughts, Tamika handed her a tin of mints. Perfect. She hurled the tin past the doorway, aiming at a metal radiator. Though the tin sailed past the radiator, it went far enough to clatter onto the linoleum hallway entrance.

A figure rushed past them, toward the inside stairwell.

It wasn't Dean Hackett. Hackett didn't sport a ponytail and didn't have a dancer's build.

"Hurry!" screeched Tamika. She ran down the hallway, tiny scissors still in her hand as if they were the Olympic torch. "Damn." She turned the knob. "It's locked from the inside. Whoever it was locked it."

"At least we can breathe for a minute." Katrina clutched her heart. "I was so prepared to stab Dean Hackett with a Pilot pen!"

Tamika bent over in peals of laughter. She held up her tiny scissors in agreement.

Katrina tore a piece of sourdough bread with her teeth. "Mmmm... that's better."

"Tell me about it." Tamika slathered her neatly cut slice with a healthy serving of olive tapenade.

"I'm so hungry I cannot even understand what the menu options are. They're a blur."

"Gnocchi is delicious. I'm ordering gnocchi."

"Perfect. And two glasses of red."

"That goes without saying."

Their server loped toward them with the easy grace of someone resigned to their fate—or about to leave work. Heavy eyebrows knit together, the server said nothing but waited, pen hovering over their pad.

Tamika looked up expectantly. "Oh? Me? Yes, I'll order the gnocchi. She'll have the same. And two glasses of your house red." She handed over the enormous floppy menus, nearly blinding Katrina. "Thanks."

The server bowed, scooched back an inch and loped away.

Katrina sighed. "Wish I was that carefree again. Or at least that clueless. I suppose both come together."

Tamika dabbed the corners of her mouth, a gesture Katrina associated only with fictional film characters.

"So besides the fact that we need to eat, why are we here? You had a definite reason for coming to this restaurant." Tamika snatched another piece of warm bread and held it aloft. "My last one. For sure."

"Carbs is what I need and carbs is what I shall eat!" declared Katrina as she chewed. "So you probably realized the figure in my office was not Dean Hackett."

"Even if he had a secret life, there's no way he could lose a hundred pounds overnight, plus gain the flexibility of a dancer."

"He's no ballerina," Katrina agreed.

"But aside from that, we don't know anything more," said Tamika. "It could have been anyone."

Katrina shook her head. "I'm way ahead of you. As soon as they ran out, I knew who it was."

"Who?" Tamika was transfixed.

"Someone who will walk in that door any minute now."

Tamika's butter knife clattered onto her plate.

Heads swiveled toward their table. Katrina's eyes fixed on one sneering woman who peered over her reading glasses at them as if she were a rigid teacher.

Katrina pointed at her. "What are you looking at?"

The teacher's glasses slid off her nose and fell into her red sauce, splattering a paint-flicked pattern all over her beautiful white silk blouse.

"No need for a scene," hissed Tamika.

"Sometimes I want to break through the passive-aggressiveness of this town."

"Well, I agree with you there." Tamika licked her lips as the server set down their glasses of red wine. "Now. Would you come to the point?"

Katrina moved her chair back and stood up. She waved her hand toward the doorway.

"Like a rabbit out of a hat. Our office burglar has arrived, right on time."

6

———

Katrina smiled as Tala approached the table. Though the student's mouth sat in a grim line, her swinging ponytail added a playfulness to her step.

"Glad you could join us, Tala. Meet Professor Scott."

Tamika offered her hand and a smile that lasted only a second. "Pleased to meet you."

Tala grinned, nodded, and moved a chair from another table. "Thank you for agreeing to meet. Under normal circumstances I'd never ask professors to meet, especially after school hours."

Tamika's shoulders relaxed.

The server materialized with their food. The tomato, garlic, oregano, and sweet onions smelled divine.

"Anything for you?" asked the server. Tala shook her head.

"She'll have a bit of mine," said Tamika, already moving some of her gnocchi to a bread plate.

"Oh, I couldn't." But Tala's eyes widened.

"Oh yes you can. I remember what it was like to be a student. Hard to get a good meal." Tamika handed her the plate.

With a temporary pang of guilt that she hadn't offered her own dish, Katrina soon focused on her food. "Let's eat and then let's talk."

After they'd inhaled their gnocchi, Katrina pushed her chair back from the table. "Now, Tala. Tell us why you were hiding in my office."

She pushed one remaining gnocchi around her plate. "What do you mean?"

Tamika set her wineglass down. "You mean you were the one in the office tonight? But why? And why did you say you had planned to meet us?"

Tala gazed at Katrina steadily, chin high. "I don't know about the office, but I did ask Professor Frost to meet here tonight."

"I'm sorry, but you're lying. Not only did I recognize your gait—which is distinctive—but your eyelid is twitching. And your hand is shaking."

Dropping her hand underneath the table, Tala sighed. "Okay, yes, I was in your office. And, yes, I pulled the fire alarm."

Tamika's eyes widened. "I hope you have a good explanation."

Another voice broke in. "I can explain."

The trio looked up.

Zeynep stood over them. A slow smirk spread across her elfin face.

"I should've realized you were behind this." Katrina pointed a fork at Zeynep.

Zeynep put up a hand to shield herself from the utensil. "It's not polite to point at people."

"Oh, sorry. You're right." Katrina placed the fork on her napkin. She and Tamika exchanged an amused glance, but Tala was busy twisting the string on her jacket around her finger.

"Will someone please tell me what is going on?" Tamika held her glass aloft.

Zeynep nodded at Tala. Tala let go of her jacket. "Zeynep had an idea this afternoon. We talked after I had been in your office, Professor Frost."

"An idea, huh?" Katrina drained her glass.

Tamika made a jabbing motion with her hand. "Let her talk, Katrina!"

"Zeynep overheard our conversation about my family being deported. She told me about her own problems with Immigration, and so I just started to pour out my heart to her. It's not normal for me to burden others, but Zeynep is a good listener."

Translation, thought Katrina: I'm not a good listener. A stab of pain rippled through her stomach.

As if she sensed Katrina's distress, Tala said, "You too are an excellent listener, Professor Frost, but you were busy. And you also haven't dealt with Immigration for your family."

"Very true," said Katrina, feeling slightly better.

"So after I was really worked up about it, I said I wanted revenge on the university for the way I was treated—in relation to the deportation issue."

Zeynep interjected. "It was actually the third or fourth time someone had mentioned revenge that day. I had thought about it myself."

"Zeynep asked me about my major, which is computer science. As soon as I mentioned the major, Zeynep's eyes lit up. I asked her why and she shook her head and said, 'It's just an idea. About revenge.'"

"And then I told her it would involve you, Professor Frost." Zeynep tucked her hair behind her ear.

"Me? Why me?"

"Because you have guts. And you have a lot of dirt on a lot of people."

Tamika nodded. "It's true. I witnessed her in action this afternoon. But how is this related to Tala breaking and entering?"

"Zeynep told me to give Professor Frost a note about meeting here tonight. Zeynep said she had an idea, but she needed time to think it over. And she needed to make a few calls. Private ones."

Katrina raised her eyebrows. "Zeynep, are you holding out on us? Who did you call?"

"The less said about those calls, the better," said Zeynep. "What I asked for, I got a big fat no. But I'm not giving up. They'll come around. Patience is bitter, but the fruit is sweet, as we say in Turkey."

Seeing that Zeynep wouldn't say more, Tala continued. "So I slipped the note under Professor Frost's door—the one inviting her here tonight. But I was still unsure."

"Unsure how?" asked Katrina.

Tala returned to twisting her jacket string around her finger. "Well…"

Katrina gave out a long, exasperated sigh.

Tamika glared at Katrina and then smiled at Tala. "Take your time."

"I wasn't sure I could trust you. My first year in college, I trusted this other professor. And she ended up telling other professors about my problem. And not in a helpful way. I got in a lot of trouble."

"Where do I come in?"

Tala stared at her knees.

Tamika cleared her throat. "I'll guess. Is it that she's a white woman professor?"

Tala nodded.

Katrina began to giggle. She would've found it all amusing anyway, but the wine surely helped.

Tala, Tamika and Zeynep stared at her.

"Are you alright?" asked Zeynep.

Katrina waved a hand in front of her face, still unable to speak. She took a deep breath. "I understand completely. It all struck me as so absurd in the moment. I didn't mean to make light of your worry. I get it."

"You do?" Tala's eyebrows knitted together in a mixture of disbelief and relief.

"Sure. But what I still don't understand is why you'd break into my office. I mean, most of my files are digital. Even if they were paper, how would you find something to confirm my trustworthiness?"

Tala shook her head. "I really don't know. I thought there'd be disciplinary files on different students…or something else." She shrugged. "I've been running on so little sleep I wasn't thinking clearly. I'm sorry." With wide doe eyes, Tala looked at Tamika and Katrina. They both nodded acknowledgment.

A phone buzzed.

Tamika held up her finger. "I'm sorry, kittens. I've got to take this." She stumbled to the front of the restaurant.

Zeynep smiled. "Kittens? How much wine has she had?"

"A glass. Must be the stress of what happened to her nephew today. Or the fact that she's a lot smaller than me." Katrina took another swig and told them the harrowing tale of Dean Hackett, Adi, and Tamika, minus the part where she'd threatened the dean.

"Hmmm." Zeynep turned over a fork on the table. "Can we trust Tamika? With a plan, I mean?"

Without a moment's hesitation, Katrina replied, "Absolutely. If she doesn't want to be a part of whatever shenanigans you have up your sleeve, she'll let us know. And will keep her mouth shut. I've been through a lot with her."

Tamika weaved back to their table. "That was the hospital."

7

"The doctor said my nephew is in stable condition. He expects a full recovery."

Katrina lifted her glass. Zeynep and Tala followed with their water glasses. "To Gabriel's full recovery. Cheers."

Though she was smiling, a single tear rolled down Tamika's cheek. She wiped it away with a napkin. "Thanks. I'm so relieved. I was at the hospital and planned to stay all day, but the nurse said I couldn't do anything. So I went to work to distract myself." She sniffed and chuckled. "And what a day it's been."

"We were about to discuss the plan," said Zeynep. "Though I'd rather not do it in a public place. I must know if you're in before I say anything else."

"Are you in, Tamika?" asked Katrina.

"Yes."

"You mean you'll say yes without hearing what it is?" asked Zeynep.

"I mean I'll hear you out. If I don't want to go along with it, I'll zip my lips. For sure. I'll do anything to get back at this university, though hopefully without losing my job."

Zeynep smiled at Katrina. "Are you in?"

Katrina nodded. "It's for my own self-protection. There are too many people after me."

"And you, Tala?"

She swallowed. "Of course."

"What's in it for you, Zeynep?" asked Tala.

Zeynep's white face drained of what little pinkness there was to begin with. "I have plenty of grievances. But I don't care to discuss them now." She pushed up her sleeves. "What's an American way to make a pact?" asked Zeynep.

"Pinky swear. Comes from Japan." Katrina held her pinky at a crooked angle. Tamika locked pinkies with Katrina. Tala and Zeynep followed.

"One question," said Katrina. "It's important."

"Yes?" Zeynep sighed.

"Can we swear?"

Zeynep smiled sweetly.

"Fuck yes."

———

Her phone vibrated against the wood floor.

Katrina groaned, grabbed the phone and threw it against the wall. She had bought an indestructible phone case for just such an eventuality.

Unfortunately, unlike old alarm clocks, this did nothing to stop the incessant buzzing.

"Ah. No, no, no, no." She half-fell, half-stumbled out of her bed. Through gritty eyes, she turned off the alarm. Then she let herself free-fall into bed.

She scrolled through a few texts absently and then stopped. Zeynep. *Meet at Katrina's house at 6 pm tonight. Bring pirate rum.*

Katrina smiled, struggled up and shuffled into the kitchen. She'd only had two glasses of wine last night but it felt like six. Must be getting old, she thought. Though thirty-eight was hardly old. She was in the prime of her life, right? Bullshit, said her inner voice. Her inner voice was a white woman with glasses and a ruler. Like an old-fashioned teacher who'd rap your knuckles for putting a comma out of place.

The earthy, sweet smell of coffee revived her as she poured a cup and sat down at the small table in her kitchen. All was quiet in this Podunk town, save the persistently cheerful birds flitting from branch to branch outside her window.

A slithering noise came from the hallway. She tiptoed around the corner. A large brown envelope lay on the floor.

Sensing she had stepped into a time warp where people used paper instead of texts, she stooped over and scooped up the envelope. The ensuing head rush sent her scurrying to the couch, though she managed not to spill a drop of precious coffee.

Katrina blinked. It was one of *those* notes. It resembled a ransom note in a movie where the culprit manages to locate a treasure trove of magazines that won't be missed.

Don't think you can get away with it. We're watching. And we will stop at nothing. Time to find another job.

Her cat, Pumpkin, a large orange beast, thumped into the living room.

"Rise and shine, sweetie." Katrina shook the threatening note in front of Pumpkin's nose. "Do you see this nonsense? They can try to scare me away, but I have tenure, dammit. I'll drive them all away before I move an inch, right, Kins?"

Pumpkin, or Kins as she often referred to him when two syllables was too much effort, rubbed his nose against the note.

"Oh, go on—side with these criminals, why don't you? I bet you'd let them into the house if they offered you some salmon, wouldn't you?"

Kins marched onto her lap, circled around twice, and then plopped down.

Rubbing his ears absently, Katrina dialed Tamika. Then she hung up abruptly. It would be better to bring the note to their meeting to find out what everyone thought. She knew if she took it to campus security they would laugh at her.

After eating a large breakfast, showering, and dressing in her suit-of-armor red wool dress, she surveyed herself in the mirror. Kins wrapped his tail around her boots. "Kins, you've covered my dress in cat hair. I demand an explanation."

Four sticky lint sheets later, she marched out of the house. She was about to walk to campus, which was almost two miles away, when a raindrop plopped on her nose.

She turned back toward her precious Fiat. The lovely seafoam-green car had been a present from her mother who believed Katrina must be chronically underpaid. She was underpaid, but not that much.

Soon she was on the road to campus, whipping past small bungalows and then larger dilapidated student housing. Enjoying the traffic-free late morning, she sped past the pharmacy, B&B, and local co-op store.

As the local news blasted from the radio, she saw, rather than heard an incoming text. Her heart began to race—it was from Jeremy, the new math professor.

Katrina tore her eyes away from the phone just in time to see the next light had changed to red.

She slammed on the brakes. Nothing happened, even though she kept pumping the pedal.

Her Fiat slid through the intersection, narrowly missing a car coming from the other direction.

"Shit, shit, shit," she screamed.

She barreled toward another intersection.

The wet pavement only made it worse.

An orange semi passed through the intersection.

She screeched and swerved around the trailer's tail end.

Fumbling around near the gear shift, she bumped her Thermos of coffee, sending it flying across her lap.

Finally, she located the emergency brake, even as her eyes were glued to the windscreen.

As she jerked the brake upward, her car slowed, but not enough to halt before the next intersection.

A Volkswagen Bug inched toward the intersection from the right.

The two cars approached as if in slow motion.

Her Fiat edged through the red light. Katrina stared at the oncoming Bug, waving her hands at the driver. Wild thoughts ran through her head. The driver had a silly, goofy smile pasted on his face. Irrationally, she fought against the thought this silly face would be the last thing she saw on earth.

The driver's face suddenly changed and he slammed on the brakes.

But not before hitting the back end of the Fiat, sending it spinning around.

And then a blessed blackness fell.

8

———

"Unit 3, Unit 3, come in."

Katrina blinked, listening to soothing radio chatter.

Police radio.

She bolted upright.

A firm hand pressed on her shoulder. "Ma'am, please lay down. You almost pulled out the IV."

"Where am I?"

"I'm Percy. And this is Heather. You've had an accident and we're going to the hospital. Please remain calm."

Percy? Where had she heard that name? Probably from her niece's train set—Thomas the Tank Engine. Percy was the shunter.

Maybe she had died and they were speeding to hell in an ambulance?

———

ADI RUSHED through the automatic doors, into the harsh fluorescent hospital lighting. Their shoes squeaked across the gleaming linoleum as they approached the front desk. The hospital may not be pretty, they thought, but it's a damn sight cleaner than Student Services.

"Good morning. I'm here to visit Katrina Frost. They told me she's in the ER."

The nurse scratched her head with a pen. "Are you family?"

"Ah, no. But she doesn't have any family in Snake's Canyon. She's a coworker."

The nurse smiled and whispered into the phone while she twirled her pen.

"You can see her now. Room 112. Just follow the red tape."

"Thanks." Adi looked down to see colored strips of tape leading in different directions, reminding them of their lovely kindergarten teacher, Miss Sanita. Adi sighed. If only one could go back to those simpler days.

Sure enough, the red tape passed by Room 112. The door was ajar.

Katrina was awake, with a petite nurse sitting by her bedside, asking, "Do you have someone who can drive you home?"

Adi walked in.

"I'll take her home. I'm a work colleague."

"Adi!" cried Katrina, flinging her arms around their candy-striped shirt.

The nurse had an unfortunate resemblance to a gargoyle, only emphasized by her deep scowl. "That's the shock. She'll be a little emotional for a while."

Tears streamed down Katrina's face. Other than a few blotches, her face was unmarked. She had a few bandages, but her wounds looked superficial. Adi let out a sigh of relief.

"What happened?" Adi sat down across from the nurse. "I drove by the accident scene and spotted Katrina. But I didn't see what happened."

Pushing back her wheeled stool, the nurse used her feet to scoot across the floor. She scooped up a folder and paddled back. "She had a lucky escape, by all accounts. If the other car had been going faster through the intersection, it would have hit the middle instead of the car's tail end. Once it hit the tail end, Ms. Frost's car spun out of control in the intersection."

"Can you tell me about her injuries?"

The nurse snapped the folder shut. "Can you give me permission to tell, sorry—what's your name?"

"Adi Tobias." Adi jiggled their leg.

"Do you, Katrina Frost, give Adi permission to hear about your diagnosis?"

Adi smiled at the wedding vow question.

Katrina nodded.

"Ms. Frost sustained minor injuries. She bumped her head, but it was mild. She's mostly experiencing emotional shock effects." She slid on her glasses and stared at her clipboard. "Symptoms include upset stomach, heart racing, tense muscles, headaches, anxiety, panic, exhaustion, and agitation. I recommend you keep her in bed and give her plenty of fluids. Treat her as if she has a bad flu."

The nurse wheeled close to Katrina and peered into her eyes. "Please tell me your birthdate, Ms. Frost. I need to confirm you're well enough to leave."

"October twenty-fifth, 1980."

Adi smiled. Though they rarely followed the zodiac that closely, Katrina's status as a Scorpio rang true. Intense, strong-willed, brilliant. A good complement to Adi's own sign, the highly sensitive Cancer.

Once she was dressed and ready, Adi gently piloted Katrina to their ancient blue Corolla.

Arms flailing, Katrina cried, "But what happened to my lovely blue Fiat?"

Adi peered at her. "It was green, Katrina. Seafoam green. C'mon. Let's get you home."

Katrina collapsed into the car and pulled at the seat belt. After three tries, it finally clicked.

The windshield wipers squeaked. Raindrops spattered the window, obscuring the gray sky and concrete.

"You good to go?" Adi asked.

"Yeah ... no. I keep getting flashbacks to the accident." Katrina shifted restlessly. "Tell me something I don't know about you. To distract me."

Adi scratched their eyebrow. "Hmmm...my life here isn't too exciting. What can I tell you?"

"A secret."

Adi laughed. "I wish I had something juicy to distract you." They paused, looking at the scar on their arm. Adi held up a finger. "I've got it. It's not exciting, but it should make you laugh."

"Well, what is it?"

"What do I watch on reruns?"

"*Fresh Prince of Bel-Air.*"

Adi chuckled. "Good guess. But it's *Golden Girls.*"

Katrina's hand flew to her mouth as she suppressed a laugh. "Excellent taste. I'd expect nothing less from you."

As they wound through Snake's Canyon backroads, Katrina said, "Why didn't you take the shortcut through town?"

Adi shifted into neutral. "Wanted to avoid the accident. No need for you to see it."

"But what have they done with my car?"

"Look!" Adi pointed at Katrina's driveway. "They must have towed it home for you."

Katrina shivered. "There's a cop car parked on the street—they probably want to talk to me."

They parked in the driveway next to her car. "Leave it to me. I'll deal with it. Sit tight."

Though Adi talked a tough game, their insides quivered. The last time they'd had a run-in with the police had been during the first week of class. A student had assaulted another student in class—a very rare occurrence—and Adi had been called in as a university representative. One police officer had been kind and polite, but the other had misgendered them, clearly on purpose, and constantly referred to Adi as a student. That was par for the course. No, what had really bothered them was the officer's rude demeanor. But what did they expect? A friendly officer?

"What are you doing?" asked Katrina.

Adi snapped their wallet shut. "I know better than to approach an officer without ID, even though this damn ID says I'm a woman." Adi clicked the door shut, sucked in a gulp of air, and marched toward the police car.

A tall police officer unfolded herself from within and ambled toward Adi, hand on her holster.

A nervous giggle noise burbled up from Adi's throat as they stood in the street, facing each other as if they were in a Western.

"Hello, Officer. I'm friends with Katrina Frost. I just brought her home from the hospital. Can I help you?"

The officer smirked. "What's your name?"

Adi handed her the ID.

With eyes wide, the officer asked, "Why did you give me your ID? Can't you tell me your name?"

"I thought it would be easier for you. You know, dispense with the formalities."

Her shoulders relaxed. "Well, your friend had a close one. She's lucky she's alive."

"Clearly." Adi inched toward the curb, realizing they could be run over in the middle of the street.

With one giant step, the officer moved closer. "No. It's not just that it was an accident—her brake lines were deliberately cut. Who wants to harm Ms. Frost? Perhaps I should interview her now." The officer moved toward Adi's car.

"Oh, no, Officer." Adi put out a hand and then let it drop. "I mean, she's on a lot of medication right now, so I doubt she could tell you anything. I'll ask her when she feels better."

"I suppose. But we'll follow up with her at some point. Tell her to call us if she remembers anything."

As the officer ambled back to her car, Adi let out a gush of air, wiggled their shoulders, and bent over, hands on knees.

"Are you alright, Adi?" called Katrina.

Adi straightened up. "Yeah, I'll be fine. Coming."

———

AFTER ADI HAD INSTALLED Katrina on the couch with plenty of blankets and tea, Katrina said, "Now, tell me about what happened with the police?"

Still feeling tense, Adi focused on Pumpkin. His fluff went a long way toward relieving stress. "I confirmed what the officer needed to know. And she told me they examined your car."

"Yes? Get on with it! Remember, I'm highly emotional."

Adi smiled and then frowned. "They said your brake lines had been cut. And they weren't frayed or anything like that. Deliberately cut."

Katrina clutched her teacup, hands trembling despite the warmth. "I'm glad they confirmed it."

"You mean you knew it?"

"Look, I didn't tell you this—mostly because it's too horrible to talk about—but I ran red lights before that intersection. I'm lucky a Beetle hit me and not the semi I narrowly missed in the intersection before it."

"Fuck," hissed Adi.

"Indeed."

"But who did it? Who'd want to kill you?"

Katrina lifted the massive Pumpkin onto her lap. He gave out a mildly irritated meow.

"I can't believe I'm saying this, but it must be someone at the university. It could be Dean Hackett, Dean Bullard, Shane Bivens. Shit. There's quite a few people who've lost their marbles and would go after me."

"Okay, I can see someone sabotaging you, but this? To kill you? It's just a university."

"You know as well as I do that especially in small towns, universities become the center of people's lives. If someone threatens your place there, it probably feels life-threatening."

"Y'all are bananas."

"Yeah, well, exactly. But it's the way it is."

Adi sipped their mint tea and blanched. "I prefer coffee." They set down the offending mug on the counter. "I guess I can imagine it. I've been so distracted, I didn't even tell you how this started out as a bad day for me and became even worse."

"How so?"

"The budget. They've threatened to cut my position next year."

Katrina waved her mug, scattering droplets all over the hapless cat. Pumpkin leapt off the couch and licked his coat sulkily.

"Sorry, Kins." She set down the mug and turned back to Adi. "That's awful. Tell me more about it."

Adi stared vacantly at the window. "Not much to tell. You know how it is—you get this bureaucratic email with a bunch of percentages outlining the different budget forecasts. Then, at the bottom, they write that your position will be cut under any of these scenarios."

Adi reflected on how many hours they had worked for the damn university over the past few years. At least seventy a week, counting all the late-night tear-stained sessions with students dealing with the many flavors of college-age problems. And during that time, despite nearly flawless annual reviews, they had received a whopping hundred-dollar raise. Once. It wouldn't have been so bad had it not been for deans and other higher-level administrators constantly misgendering them, not out of ignorance, but out of malice. One associate dean had asked "what kind of people" Adi dated. Adi had experienced this question enough that they had retorted, "Definitely not anyone like you." Predictably, this comment had led to a series of passive-aggressive punishments and shunning from other administrators.

"Adi? Are you there?" Katrina paused. "They didn't even have the decency to call you or meet in person?"

"Nope. And honestly, it's probably better this way because I'd rather not get angry at someone for it."

"Well, I'm angry at someone. A whole lotta someones."

9

———————

After a restless day of puttering about, eating chocolate ice cream, checking emails, and eating chocolate ice cream again, it was time for Katrina to go to Zeynep's house for their meeting. Taking the text about bringing pirate's rum to heart, she poked around in her over-filled cupboards to find an ancient, dust-covered bottle of rum. She blew on it, coughed, and read the card looped around its neck with a gold cord. *Dear Professor Frost—From my hometown. Thank you for everything. Anthony.*

Perfect! A vague picture surfaced of a tall, lanky young international student from the Dominican Republic. With a jolt, she remembered how he had made a complaint against Public Safety and had been called into the dean's office. She had blocked out the memory, yet another reminder of how the administration had increased its nastiness quotient over the past five years. It had happened slowly, sometimes so slowly it was hard to recognize. But it was there.

Her phone buzzed. *I'm outside.* A text from Adi.

Katrina threw the bottle into her bag, slid on a warm coat and laughed at Pumpkin. "Look at you, sweet baby. You have chocolate ice cream all over your face!" Pumpkin probably shouldn't lick the ice cream bowl. But, hey, life was short.

The rain had turned again to a fine mist, but this time there was a biting chill in the air. A neighbor's carved pumpkin flickered grinned evilly at her from across the street. It reminded her of the leer on Hackett's face yesterday. She shook her head and told herself this was not the time to lose it.

"Thanks for picking me up, Adi. And I didn't properly thank you for everything you did this morning. I'm not sure how I would have made it home."

"Oh, you'd have made it home, but I'm glad I was there to handle the police officer." Adi's leg jiggled.

"Me too." Katrina paused. "Are you nervous about something?"

Adi looked down at their leg and grinned. "Mostly just a habit. But, yes, I'm anxious about my job. And, well, everything. But it's normal for me."

They drove on in companionable silence until they reached Zeynep's small bungalow on the outskirts of town. Zeynep was proud of the renovated house and little vegetable and flower garden around the back. She had bought it five years ago after finishing her master's degree in North Carolina. At the time, it had been a ramshackle mess, but she had soon renovated it, piece by piece, until it exuded a warm charm, unlike many of the other houses on the street.

As they got out of the car, the door to the house opened, revealing a small wiry figure silhouetted in the glow of candlelight.

"Batu! You're back!" cried Katrina.

The baby-faced Batu grinned and held out his arms. "*Hoşgeldiniz.* Welcome, Katrina. And Adi—I haven't seen you in years."

They exchanged hugs as Batu ushered them out of the foul weather. "Just got in from Berlin last week. Fortunately, the weather seems to be about the same."

"Are you staying for long?" asked Adi as they struggled to take off their coat.

"Perhaps. Now that my fellowship's all finished, I'm looking for a job."

"Aren't we all," mumbled Adi.

"Sorry? What did you say?"

"Oh, nothing," said Adi, plastering a false smile across their face. "What kind of job do you want?"

"Maybe something in student affairs? I don't know. Anything so I can paint."

And paint he did. Batu's colorful paintings, mixed with serious sepia canvases, littered the walls of Zeynep's house.

"Ah. You've arrived!" Zeynep gave them each double air-kisses and led them into the living room.

Tala and Tamika sat chatting by a cheery fire. They waved at Adi and Katrina. Owls littered the fireplace mantel. Carved owls, knitted owls, plush toy owls, plastic owls.

Tamika waved a hand at Zeynep. "I have a question for you."

"Sounds serious," said Zeynep.

Katrina smiled. "Tamika always has questions."

Ignoring Katrina, Tamika continued. "Tala and I were curious about the owls on the mantelpiece. Do they mean something?"

Zeynep put her hands on her hips, elbows akimbo. She was trying to be serious, but she soon broke into giggles.

Tamika's eyes slewed to Tala and then to Katrina.

"No, no. I found it funny because I had to be so serious at work today. Owls are my weakness. Since I was a child. I adore them."

Katrina furrowed her brow. "But you're always so serious, Zeynep. Are you saying it's an act for work?"

She nodded. "Yes, I'm actually rather a silly person."

"Oh, go on," said Tamika.

"No, really. I am."

"Well, I suppose your request for pirate's rum does prove it." Katrina rummaged around in her bag and pulled out the bottle of rum. "Ta-da! This was the best I could do."

Zeynep's face broke into a delighted grin. She waved her poet sleeves about. "Look, Katrina brought pirate's rum."

"I was wondering about your text," said Tamika. "Why pirate's rum?"

"You'll see," said Zeynep mysteriously as she disappeared into the kitchen.

"Are you old enough to drink, Tala?" asked Adi.

"Ever the student affairs person, aren't you?" laughed Tamika.

"Don't worry, Adi," said Tala. "I'm twenty-one. About to graduate from this ridiculous university."

"I'll toast to that," said Zeynep as she reappeared with a tray of glasses, olives, cheese, and bread.

"I'll join you all for a toast and will leave you to your mysterious plans." Batu winked.

Katrina raised her glass, "To this ridiculous university and Tala's graduation!"

They all clinked.

Adi continued, "And to Katrina surviving an accident this morning."

Everyone's smiling faces faded as they lowered their glasses.

"What happened, Professor Frost?" Tala gulped.

Katrina sighed. "Would you tell them, Adi? I want to save my strength for the good part of the evening."

After Adi had finished the tale, Zeynep slammed her glass of rum on the table. "Well, that's it. No more barking up the wrong wood."

"Tree," corrected Tala gently.

"Thank you, Tala. Tree." She inhaled. "Are you all ready to discuss our plan for revenge?"

"More ready than you'll ever know," sighed Tamika.

Batu drained his glass, set it down and clapped his hands together. "Right. If you need me for any of your revenge plans, I'll be taking my own revenge on a canvas in the basement." He trotted off, whistling as he went.

10

———

"Your brother is precious," said Tamika.

And handsome. Katrina's heart gave a little lurch.

"He is a dear. And makes the house less lonely, especially when Findik goes out to play."

A fat tabby waddled into the center of the living room and leapt onto the footstool in the center of the room. He began to lick himself contentedly, holding court without glancing at his subjects.

"Don't give Findik any of your rum. That cat is a budding alcoholic." She rubbed him between the ears and grabbed a stack of papers sitting on the table. "Now, I have something for each of you." They all passed around folders with their names until everyone had the right one.

"Are these our secret dossiers?" laughed Tamika.

"Of a kind."

"Should we read them now?" Katrina popped a dried fig into her mouth. Delicious. Though she couldn't say anything further as her whole mouth was now preoccupied.

Zeynep nodded. "Skim them. Then tell everyone your story."

"Yes, Professor Zaman." Adi's mouth was full of tabouli.

Katrina scanned her sheet of paper. Her eyebrows lifted. "Sadie the Goat? What does that have to do with me?"

"Go ahead, read it." Tamika removed her glasses. "Mine is about someone named Sayyida al-Hurra."

Katrina cleared her throat. "Sadie, apparently, was deceptively fierce for her small stature. It says here that she and her partner—a man—would pick out a target, and then Sadie would sneak up on him and head-butt him in the guts. While he was still recovering, her partner would hit him on the head and take all his money."

Adi chuckled. "You head-butted Dean Hackett yesterday."

Tala's eyes grew wide.

"Metaphorically speaking, of course," Adi finished.

Ignoring Adi's comment, Katrina went on. "It says she became the head of a male pirate gang in New York City. They stole a boat and sailed upriver, looting mansions along the way."

"Why did she leave New York?" asked Tala.

"It says Sadie's nemesis was a woman named 'Gallus Mag' who ran a bar. She wouldn't tolerate bad behavior. If anyone acted up, she'd bite their ear off. And all the ears were stashed in a pickle jar that sat on top of the bar. Sadie got on her wrong side, apparently, and lost an ear. But at least she had the honor of seeing the ear get its very own jar, marked 'Sadie.'"

Absently, Katrina put her left hand up to her ear. It was still there. "What does yours say, Tamika?"

Tamika slid her glasses back on. "Sayyida al-Hurra was known as the pirate queen of the Mediterranean in the late 1400s. Unlike many pirates, she took to the sea to build her community. Her family fled Spain after Christians took control. According to the dossier, she vowed revenge against the Spanish for all the pain they'd caused. Oh, and Sayyida wasn't her real name. It's Arabic for 'a lady who is free and independent.'"

"Ooo...I like that," said Tala.

"She had a long and successful career, apparently. For twenty years, she more or less controlled half the Mediterranean. She poured the money from her pirating back into her home in North Africa."

Tamika sat back, tapping one arm of her reading glasses against her cheek. "What is this all about, Zeynep?"

Zeynep rubbed her index finger and thumb together, a sure sign she was in deep thought. Then she winked at Tamika. "Don't worry. I'll tell you as soon as Tala and Adi finish. Then I'll explain my dossier."

Adi rose and wandered around the room, as if they were rehearsing their new lead role. "Gunpowder Gertie, born in 1879, was a Canadian pirate. As a penniless orphan, she found she couldn't make money as a woman, so decided to do so as a man. After losing her eye in an explosion while working as a coal hand on a steamboat, the doctor who attended her told the crew she was a woman. Not surprisingly, she was fired. Seeking revenge, she somehow conned the Canadian police into giving her a ship. She named it the Tyrant Queen—"

"Sounds like an eighties band," sighed Katrina.

Adi glared and held up a hand. "Please. Do not break my flow."

Katrina bowed.

"The Tyrant Queen, flying a Jolly Roger flag, made a great deal of money. Until one day, a man on her crew betrayed her to the police. She was captured and sentenced to life in prison, where she died in 1912."

Paper in hand, Adi curled up on the sofa next to Zeynep. "I hope someone else has a happier ending. I was all in until the last part!"

Tala leapt up. "My dossier is a couple of pages, but I'll do my best to summarize. Jacquotte Delahaye's parents were Haitian or Spanish. Either way, she lived her whole life in the Caribbean. When she was a child, the Spanish killed her parents in front of her. Like some of the other pirates, she swore revenge. To make things easier, she began dressing as a man. Some people say she only took up the male disguise after faking her own death in a fight. It's surprising she wasn't immediately discovered because she still had the bright red hair that had always been her trademark. Eventually people started to call her 'Back from the Dead Red' because of it."

"How did she end up?" asked Adi.

Tala flipped to the next page. "She died in a shoot-out with the Spanish in the 1660s. It was three against one."

Adi groaned.

"However! She commanded one hundred men on her ship and remained a loner her whole life. It says here that she symbolizes all pirates in any era, men and women, in her desire for freedom."

"Impressive." Katrina sipped her rum. "And how about Zeynep? Do you have a pirate?"

"Of course." She slid her legs underneath her and leaned one arm against the back of the couch. "My pirate is Ching Shih. She was the most ruthless pirate of all time."

"When was she born?" asked Tala.

"1775. In Guangdong Province in China. According to this article, she stood up for her fellow women. Even the prisoners: if a woman captive was attacked, her attacker would get it in the neck. And if he dared to marry one, and then cheated on her or hurt her, he might even get the death penalty. It wasn't only rapists and wife-beaters Ching went after, though. Any thieves among her employees were liable to get their heads chopped off, and deserters would lose their ears."

Tamika covered one ear. "What is this obsession with ears tonight? First Sadie and now Ching Shih." She munched on a dried apricot. "Don't tell me. The police captured her and she died in prison."

Zeynep smiled. "No. That's one of the benefits of ending the stories with this pirate. She died at the ripe old age of sixty-nine in 1844."

"In prison, right?" asked Tala.

"No. She died in her own bed, surrounded by family."

The mood became considerably brighter. Chatter and laughter broke out. Batu padded in from the hallway. He had a paintbrush behind his ear. "Why all the noise? Am I missing a party?"

Zeynep laughed. "You're looking for an excuse to stop working on your painting."

Batu gave them all a sheepish grin. "It's true. It's these ears. Human ears are so difficult to paint."

"Maybe your subject lost theirs in a pirate battle," said Adi. Everyone started laughing.

Eyebrows lifted, Batu shook his head. "You've all caught a cold in the head."

"He means we've all gone crazy. It's a Turkish idiom," explained Zeynep.

"Call me when you decide to drink raki." He turned and shuffled away.

A phone buzzed. Tamika picked up her sleek black Android and tapped it with her well-manicured finger. "We'd better make this quick. I need to visit my nephew in the hospital. He says he wants to tell me something."

She chuckled to herself. "And he wants me to bring him a slice of his favorite chocolate cake."

Zeynep nodded. "We've all had grievances against this university, which is normal at any university, I suppose. But lately, it's really out of control. I've invited you all because you all have a grievance. Tala has her mistreatment and the mistreatment of her parents, Adi's losing their job, Katrina was nearly killed today, and Tamika's nephew is in the hospital."

"What about you?" asked Adi.

"I've got plenty of grievances. Let's say they're cumulative."

She's playing this close to her chest, isn't she, thought Katrina.

"So it's time for revenge. And not a simple revenge, but one that really gets our point across. And has a cause attached to it," said Zeynep.

Tala shifted in her seat. "What did you have in mind?"

"I have an idea. And a connection that may be able to help make it happen—if I can bring them on board. But I'm not sure about the details."

Adi scratched their head. "I dunno. Is this a good idea? Revenge? Isn't it very shaming?"

"Oh, c'mon, Adi. You've got to let go of student-development-speak. This is real. People are getting hurt. I was almost killed today. These greedy nutcases have to be stopped."

Waving her dossier, Tamika said, "I'm all in. I've had it." She slid her reading glasses further down her nose and peered at Zeynep. "Are you proposing we rob them? Or hurt them?"

Zeynep shook her head. "We women pirates—or let's say non-cis-men."

"Hey—I like queens," said Adi.

"Okay, we pirate queens of the twenty-first century are more sophisticated than that. We'll meet tomorrow night once I've got these other details worked out."

Katrina rose to her feet. She raised her glass of rum. Everyone rose and stood in a circle.

"To the pirate queens of Snake's Canyon."

11

———

Tamika's eyes strayed from the road as she heard the cake tin clattering open yet again. A quick glance over to the passenger seat confirmed her suspicions. "Mm-hmm," mumbled Katrina, "this chocolate cake is delicious. You should give me the recipe."

Tamika shifted gears. "But you don't bake. Why do you want the recipe?"

"True. It seems like the right thing to say."

"Well, make sure you don't eat all of it. Gabriel needs to keep his strength up."

"With cake?" Katrina paused. "What am I saying? Of course with cake. Lots of protein from those eggs. And iron from the chocolate."

As the Mini slid into the parking space, Tamika grabbed Katrina's hand.

"Ow. What is it?"

"Sorry. I've been losing it over the past couple of days."

"Tell me about it. This morning nearly put me over the edge."

"See?" Tamika rubbed her eyes. "I even forgot you nearly died this morning." She set her head against the wheel, as if that would stop the thoughts spinning around in her head. Gabriel. Katrina. Her job

—did she really want it anymore? The poisonous university. Dean Hackett's smirk.

Tamika sighed and lifted her head. "Can you keep an eye on me when we're in there? I'm not sure if I'll go to pieces or chew out a doctor. Anything is possible."

Patting Tamika's hand, Katrina said. "Sure. I'll say 'chocolate' if you need to snap out of it, okay? Though don't be too sure I'm not the one who will lose it."

"Guess we have to be badass pirate queens now, don't we?"

As Tamika inspected her teeth in the rearview mirror for any traces of cake, she saw a black Porsche screech into a tight spot behind them. She craned her neck. The door opened and a penny loafer with a tassel appeared.

"Oh my God. Get down or he'll spot us!" Tamika slid down in her seat.

"Why? What's gotten into you?" Despite her protest, Katrina slid down as well.

"It's Dean Hackett. It has to be. I'd recognize those shoes anywhere."

"What are you talking about? What shoes?"

"C'mon. Let's follow him."

They slid out of the car, gently clicking their doors into place. They ran, hunched over, to the elevator. Sure enough, Dean Hackett's mane of hair flapped in the gentle breeze as he waited for the elevator.

He turned toward them.

Tamika waved at Katrina and they each leapt to one side, right in front of the entrance to the elevator vestibule.

Tamika heard a cough. Then the unmistakable sound of a flicking lighter. So he was a secret smoker, too. She remembered last year's convocation, when the president had announced the campus was smoke-free. Dean Hackett had sat behind him, cheering him on. As an occasional smoker herself, she had to admit she had cheered on the president too, with the irrational hope that a smoke-free campus would finally help her kick the habit. Though weed smoking was more of an issue than cigarettes these days. She had to tell her students to cut back.

Tamika tapped frantically at her phone.

Once the cigarette odor had faded and the elevator door closed, they stepped into the vestibule. Tamika smashed her fist against the button at least twenty times.

"Who were you texting?" asked Katrina, inhaling the bit of cigarette smoke left behind.

"Gabriel. I don't know if they've allowed him to have his phone, but I told him to act normally if Dean Hackett showed up."

"What does 'act normally' mean?"

"I have no idea, but it seemed like the right thing to do." Tamika stared at the glowing elevator buttons, lost in a nostalgic reverie of Gabriel's childhood. He'd always been a sweetie, even if his insatiable curiosity had led him to stick things in light sockets. And now. And now, here he was in the hospital because of...a suicide attempt. Tamika felt mildly ashamed somehow, despite her better judgment. When the image of Dean Hackett wandered into her consciousness, her fists clenched. This university. Someone or something had driven her sweet Gabriel to this. And dammit, they would pay.

Ding.

With a gentle flop of her stomach, they reached the third floor. Katrina put a hand on her shoulder. "Don't worry, Tamika. We'll get there soon enough."

Tamika wiped away a tear and waved Katrina on behind her. "Follow me. He's in room 301C."

They tiptoed down the shiny linoleum hallway. It was preternaturally quiet for a hospital. Tamika glanced at a wall clock. Midnight. Would the nurses let them in? But the nurses weren't at their station, so she straightened up and sauntered through the hallway with all the confidence of a doctor.

"Wait!" hissed Katrina. "The dean—it's his footsteps."

The distinctive shuffling followed by a quickstep grew louder.

They glued themselves to the wall. The dean shuffled by the hallway perpendicular to them.

"Let's go," whispered Tamika.

"Why? Are we going to confront him?"

"Hell yes, we are. I want him to know we noticed him."

They ran down the hall, skidded around the corner and came to a halt in front of 301C, marked with a cheery whale on the door. Why did hospital management believe that the inhumanity of the fluorescent lights, disinfectant, and paternalism would be washed away by a grinning plastic whale?

They stood sentry on either side of the door. Tamika touched her ear and leaned in closer.

Silence.

No voices. No footsteps.

The door wasn't thick enough to block out noise. So it really was quiet.

Tamika frowned. She knocked on the door.

Hearing the rustling of bedclothes was a relief.

A mumbled "Come in" prompted Tamika to push open the door.

Gabriel lay against a bank of puffy pillows, reading *From Amo to Táíwò*. His furrowed brow relaxed as he saw them.

"Auntie Ta!" He grinned. A dimple formed on one side of his chubby cheeks, completing his cherubic appearance. His close-cropped hair with two fade lines provided structure to his soft form. He pushed himself up further and smoothed the sheets. Tamika let out an uncharacteristic squeak of relief.

His sweet grin turned to a look of alarm. "But what are you doing here so late?"

"What are you doing reading so late?"

"Oh, this. It's for a paper. The book is so good though, I couldn't stop. I've been asleep all day." His eyes slewed to the side. "Who's this?"

Katrina stepped forward with her hand outstretched, as if she were meeting the president. "Professor Frost. You can call me Katrina."

He eyed her up and down. "I've heard of you. You're a tough grader, aren't you?"

Katrina sighed.

"Kidding," he laughed. "I've heard only good things about you. Except if someone gets on your bad side."

"Glad you're better, sweetie." Tamika sat on the bed and patted his leg. She turned to Katrina. "He's the joker of the family. He's clearly improved."

She paused. It wouldn't be right to stress him out, but she had to know what was going on. "Listen, honey. Did anyone just come in here now?"

"A nurse came by a half hour ago."

"No, not a nurse. A dean."

His eyes widened. "Why would a dean visit me? And at midnight? I know I'm in trouble and everything, but..." He trailed off.

"Maybe you fell asleep and then heard a knock?" asked Katrina.

Gabriel shook his head. "Nope. I've been reading."

They all sighed.

"Wait!" He held up a hand. "I did hear footsteps stop outside my door. But nothing else."

Tamika glanced at the door. A white envelope, hardly visible against the white linoleum, sat behind the door. She scooped it up and automatically handed it to Gabriel. Then she snatched it back.

"Hey! It's for me."

"I know. But I'm worried about what's in it. Let me have a peek first."

Katrina peered over Tamika's shoulder.

She gasped.

Gabriel sat bolt upright. "What the—"

Katrina pointed. "It's the same janky lettering from the note someone put under my door this morning!" She scrabbled around in her bag and produced the crumpled note.

They moved to the table and laid out the two notes next to each other.

"It's like a ransom note." Tamika couldn't stop the quiver in her voice.

Gabriel pushed himself toward the end of the bed, wincing. "What does it say?"

"Sorry, sweetie." Tamika licked her lips and glanced at Katrina.

Katrina nodded. "It says you'd better keep quiet—or else."

Gabriel scrunched up his face and buried his head in the bank of pillows. Soft whimpers floated up from the bed.

A knock came at the door.

Just as Katrina went to open it, the door swung open.

12

"Ow!" Katrina yelped. The door hit her hard in the knee.

A nurse, clad in clogs and blue scrubs, peered down at the crumpled Katrina.

"Didn't your mother ever tell you it's dangerous to sit near doors, young lady?"

Katrina looked at her in disbelief.

"Well, don't sit there, stand up." She eyed Katrina and Tamika. "What are you two doing here after hours? The patient needs rest."

Gabriel's tear-stained face appeared from behind the pillows. "My name is Gabriel, not patient."

A flash of pride spread across Tamika's face, but it soon disappeared. "I'm Gabriel's aunt. And we have reason to believe he may be in danger."

The nurse's glasses, attached to a chain, slid off her blotchy pink nose and swung about her shrunken frame. "This isn't *Law and Order*, miss. We're in Snake's Canyon, remember?"

"It's Doctor. Dr. Tamika Scott."

"If you're a doctor, why don't you attend to him yourself?"

Enough was enough. Katrina pulled herself up and loomed over the nurse. "May I have your name and ID number, please, Nurse—"

"Nurse Emeline Beech. B-e-e-c-h. Like a beech tree. Number 48912."

This one was a beech alright, thought Katrina.

Nurse Beech slid her glasses back into place. "And you're welcome to report me to whomever you want, but they won't get rid of me. There's a severe shortage of nurses."

She spun on her clogged heel and marched out of the room.

Gabriel sighed. "At least she's gone."

"Honey, you must tell us what that note meant." Tamika tidied the covers.

"I-I-I dunno."

"Look, Gabriel. I don't know you, but you've been bamboozled. I'm fairly certain the note I received this morning"—she pointed at the table—"was from the same person who delivered your note." She paused. "And I'm guessing the poison pen was Dean Hackett."

Gabriel's eyes widened. He ran his front teeth over the bottom of his lip. "Yes. Although I don't know if it was the dean or not. I know it was some person who works for the university."

Tamika rubbed her eyes. "Let's begin at the beginning."

"I need some coffee," sighed Katrina.

"There's some instant in the corner if you want it. One of the nurses brought in a hot water kettle and some coffee earlier. She forgot it."

"Blech," said Tamika.

"It'll do." Katrina switched on the kettle and peered into the dubious tin labeled "coffee."

Gabriel folded his hands and laid them against his soft mound of a stomach. "It's like this. Professor Frost doesn't know this, but I'm a journalist for the *Blipton University Observer*."

"Oh! So you're Gabriel Lomax. The *Observer* is usually crap, but your stories are actually good."

He grinned. "Thanks. Anyway, I started a story on the new dorms they're building on the edge of campus. I interviewed a few people at the Center for Community Interfacing—"

"Or, as I call it, the Center for Saving University Face." Katrina poured hot water into her cup and stirred.

Tamika shot her a warning glance.

"So Sally Spriggs, who works at the center, told me about how people in the neighborhood were upset about the new dorms because the project is driving the price of rent up. Landlords are pushing up their rent and people who've lived their whole lives there are being driven out."

Katrina and Tamika nodded.

Gabriel rubbed his left temple. "I was already aware of the situation, of course. But I had a gut feeling something else was going on. So I asked Sally about the developer for the land—Aragon Partners. Something flashed across her face and she fell silent. Then she tripped over her words and told me she was busy. I sensed I was onto something."

"And?"

"And there's a Blipton trustee who used to work for Aragon Partners. This same trustee was on the board when the contract went through for the dorm. He still is on the board of trustees."

Katrina let out a low whistle.

Tamika shook her head. "But this kind of thing happens all the time. It's a small town. Relatively speaking."

Gabriel smiled. "I had the same thought. I wrote it up in my journalism class and presented it at the end of the semester. I received a positive response, so I told a few people I would publish it in the school newspaper. My journalism professor encouraged me to talk to the *Snake's Canyon Times* instead, so I did."

Katrina screwed up her face. "This coffee is awful."

Gabriel smiled. "I told you."

Katrina downed the lot like she was taking a shot of cold medicine. "Sorry. Go on."

"As soon as I talked to the *Times*, strange things started happening. One day, I walked into my door room and noticed my papers were out of place. I asked our resident assistant about it and she said she hadn't been in there—the RAs are the only ones allowed to go into our rooms. Then my email account stopped working. And some of my files on the university server disappeared."

Gabriel's eyes turned glassy. "Then I received a typed letter—a regular letter, not in that weird ransom note lettering. It said if I published the story—they didn't say what it was, but I guessed—my family would suffer for it. And whoever wrote it was clear they meant physical harm."

"Do you still have the letter?" asked Katrina.

He shook his head. A single tear trickled down his face. "I burned it, though I couldn't even do that right. I set off the fire alarm."

Tamika grabbed his hand. "Shhh...sweetie, you didn't do anything wrong."

"The note said not to go to the police." He snorted and wiped away the tear. "As if I would. I don't want to get shot."

Katrina and Tamika waited patiently.

Gabriel sniffed. "The problem was, I'd already sent the story to the paper. I called and emailed day and night, but no one would answer me. Finally, I got a call from a journalist I didn't know and she said they were publishing the story the next day. I begged her not to do it, but she said they didn't need my permission."

"So you tried to...." Tamika trailed off.

"The fact that you might get hurt, Auntie, was the final straw. I was already so depressed. I didn't have many friends and ever since the Aragon Partners story came into my life, I felt like I became more and more paranoid. I pushed away the few friends I did have. It was all so hopeless."

Katrina nodded sympathetically. She couldn't imagine ever taking her own life, but she understood depression. And the emotional highs and lows of one's early twenties.

A long thin nose poked around the door. Nurse Beech.

"Visiting hours are over. Don't make me call security."

13

***

Katrina couldn't breathe.

Something lay heavy on her chest.

Dean Hackett.

Her eyes fluttered open. It had been a dream, but she still couldn't breathe.

Yellow eyes glowed back at her in the darkness.

"Pumpkin!"

She rolled over, dislodging the large block of fur onto the bed and then onto the floor. Pumpkin glared up at her.

"How many times have I told you not to sit on my chest, you silly vegetable!"

With a flick of his tail, Pumpkin marched into the hallway.

"Good riddance," she groaned, flopping back over on her side.

A knock came at the door.

Katrina drifted back lightly into a warm fuzzy dream.

Then banging.

She sat up, completely awake now. Her heart was racing. No one ever knocked on her door at nine in the morning, much less banged on it. What if someone was here to hurt her?

Now in her pink fluffy robe, she rummaged around in her nightstand. A nail file. That would do the trick. She slid it into her pocket. Her old confidence returned and she marched to the door.

"Who is it?"

"Zeynep."

The opened door revealed a sopping wet Zeynep. Her bike was propped up against the side of the house.

"What are you doing?"

Without waiting for an answer, Katrina pulled Zeynep into the house. She disappeared momentarily, returning with another pink fluffy robe and a towel. "Here, use these."

"I'll be alright."

Katrina knew Zeynep was as stubborn as herself. "It's freezing out there and you're soaked. Not a choice, it's an order. I don't want you dripping all over the furniture. Neither does Pumpkin."

Pumpkin watched from a safe distance. He started to meow.

"Yes, yes, Kins. I'll feed you soon." She turned to Zeynep. "I'll feed the beastie and you dry your hair."

After the cat had been satisfied and Katrina had made two cups of coffee with special foam, she and Zeynep settled on the couch.

"Now. Don't tell me. Adi came here yesterday to tell me they had been laid off. Not you, too?"

"No. I heard about Adi through the grapevine, unfortunately." She grimaced. "I rushed over here because I didn't want to use the phone or email. The police came to our door after you all left last night."

Katrina involuntarily squeezed Pumpkin's fat hind leg. He waddled to Zeynep's lap.

Zeynep pulled her wet bobbed hair behind her ear. "They said they were investigating a series of incidents on campus—"

"What incidents?"

"No clue. I thought it might have been the fire alarm yesterday, but it's not enough to get the local police involved."

"You think it's an excuse? What, to watch you? Or Batu?"

Zeynep shrugged and patted Pumpkin's head. "I don't know. We've had Immigration at our door before, so anything's possible."

"I don't remember that—did you tell me about it and I forgot?"

"We weren't that close at the time, so I doubt I told you. Actually, Batu and I were living separately at the time, but obviously I was the one who visited him in detention. We never found out why they really detained him."

"What do you mean? They didn't tell you?"

"They said something was wrong with his student visa, but as far as I could see, everything was in order. I suspect they were looking for someone who fit his profile—loosely, of course—and detained him for that reason. After it happened a second time, I said he should live with me. He was low on cash and I said it would look less suspicious than him living on his own. Sweetheart that he is, he said he didn't want to intrude or take my money. I finally convinced him and he's quite happy painting away in his studio."

Zeynep sighed. "Given those past experiences, we must limit our communication via text, phone, and email."

"Understood. Anything else?"

"There's been a development. The university is putting on a trustee gala event tonight, and I got hold of the attendee list. I want you to go."

"Tonight? By myself?"

"No. With Tamika and Tala. It'll be part of the plan."

"You and your plans. Can't you tell me?"

"I'll tell you all later this afternoon. We're meeting again. Though I think it's better if we meet at Adi's place."

"Why?"

"I know Tamika has some family staying with her, and I don't think our places are safe right now. And Tala lives in the dorms."

Katrina shivered.

"Okay, okay, I'm happy to do what's needed. But it's so last-minute. How will the three of us get invited to this gala?"

"You forget my magic administrative assistant skills, Professor Frost. I've arranged to have the three of you invited already."

"What about you and Adi? Will you be there?"

"I've arranged for us to be there to help out with decorations, catering, and the like. We're both cleared to be food handlers."

"But how will we let the others know about our plans?"

"You can text Tala and tell her you want to meet about her paper—then give her the address."

"If the police are tracking us, they'll probably think we're having an affair."

"I doubt it. Male professors arrange to meet with their students off campus, even if they don't have libidinous intent. They think nothing of it."

"What about Tamika and Adi?"

"I'll tell Adi in person since we have a meeting later this morning. And as for Tamika, are you going to see her today?"

"I know she teaches today. I do too, so I'll try to find her in her office."

Zeynep rose from the couch and drained her coffee. She looked so much like a pixie in her bright green jumpsuit Katrina half-expected her to fly away.

Pumpkin took advantage of the extra couch space and stretched all the way across a cushion. Zeynep stared at him and said in a forced casual voice, "There's one more thing."

Katrina groaned. "There had to be."

"I received an urgent email telling me to tell you to go to Dean Bullard's office. At ten."

"But I teach my class at ten fifteen!"

"He said you should cancel whatever you had on, even if it was a class."

With a shaking hand, Katrina pulled back her long hair from around her face. "It's nine now. I'd better take a shower and..."

"What?" asked Zeynep.

"My car isn't working. I'll need to walk."

"You can bike with me."

"You know I dislike it. You arrive on campus all perfect as usual. But I arrive as a hot mess, with my hair flying everywhere and clothes dirty."

"The rain's stopped. It's either take a shower and then bike, or walk and no shower."

"Alright. Biking it is."

"I'll wait for you. I'll drink the rest of the coffee."

"Hey! I wanted another cup!"

"You'd better not. Your whole body is shaking."

14

———

The lipstick tube rolled off the counter and onto the floor. Behind the toilet.

"Fuck. Fucking goddamn day." Katrina's swearing echoed in the tiled university bathroom. There was no way she was reaching behind the filthy toilet. She brushed her frizzy hair, which seemed to only increase the frizz, and then decided to put everything up in a bun. The result in the mirror was rather lopsided, but it would have to do. After all, why was she trying to make herself presentable for Dean Cauliflower-Ear-Brain Bullard?

She pushed her makeup pouch back into her capacious bag, plastered on a fake smile in the mirror and marched out of the bathroom, across to the dean's office.

A few yellowed higher education magazines sat on the table, next to today's *Snake's Canyon Times*. The headline read: "Cozy relationships between developers and university." Good God. Must be Gabriel's story. The dean was sure to be in a bad mood. Fantastic.

"Can I help you, Professor Frost?"

"Thanks, Sammy. I'm here to meet Dean Bullard."

"Oh, yes, of course. He said you'd be coming." Sammy looked down.

Sweet Jesus. This was going to be a fun day.

A door opened from somewhere in the wing. Dean Bullard trundled out, licking his fingers. "Do we have any more of those donuts, Sammy?"

"Yes, Dean Bullard." Sammy produced a plate with an assortment of donuts from the best bakery in town. Top Donut. Katrina would recognize them anywhere. Especially that glazed maple bar.

Dean Bullard slid two donuts onto his plate. Without asking permission, Sammy offered the plate to Katrina.

What the hell. Sugar was needed in these dire circumstances. "Thanks, Sammy. The maple bar is my favorite."

"Me too!"

Dean Bullard gawked at the two of them as if they'd said they enjoyed eye of newt.

In between chomps, Dean Bullard said, "Follow me, Katrina. Thanks for coming. I know you had a class."

"It's alright. They're working in groups today. They're doing research on institutional oppression in the university."

"Mhhh..." Dean Bullard nodded and plopped down at the oval table next to his desk.

The man couldn't give a rat's ass about anything. He didn't even understand the irony of her class assignment.

"Now, Katrina." He wiped his hands on one of those pieces of wax paper that get passed off as napkins.

"Yes?" Katrina sank her teeth into the maple bar. Heaven.

"I called you in because there have been some developments regarding the matter we spoke about yesterday. We have a leak on the rank and tenure committee. You'll remember I told you about Shane Bivens accusing you of tampering with the rank and tenure results? Well, the investigation is in full swing now. I'd like to ask you a few questions."

Katrina leveled her best withering gaze at him. "Please do."

Dean Bullard leaned back in his chair, groping for something on the desk. His short arms were not up to the job, so he got up and rooted around the top of his desk, which seemed to be layered in brown campus envelopes. Two were from Dean Hackett.

He found a tablet with a small keyboard and held it up in triumph. "Okay. Let's start with the accusation." His stubby fingers flew across the keyboard. "Shane says he suspects you of telling Quincy about the outcome of his tenure vote."

"How would he know? Does he have any proof if he's going to make an accusation? After all, the man drinks vodka at our rank and tenure meetings."

Dean Bullard let out something between a sigh and a snort. His nose was so full of hair the sound sounded muffled and reedy. "You don't know that for sure, Katrina."

"Are you serious? What? I smelled alcohol on his breath, so I smelled his coffee mug."

"Lots of people keep a bottle of Jim Beam in their offices," he said indulgently.

Katrina leaned forward, struggling not to roll her eyes. "But not to drink at nine in the morning at an important committee meeting."

"Let's get back to the issue at hand. Shane says Associate Dean Cheryl Chalmers had a conversation with Quincy. Quincy was apparently very upset about the whole process because he had found out his department didn't support his candidacy. While he was in her office, he revealed he was even more upset at finding out the rank and tenure committee didn't support him either."

"Did he say where he got this information?"

"No."

"Well, then, why are we here?"

"Cheryl reported her conversation—as she should have—to Shane as head of the committee and to me as dean."

Fucking backstabbing bitch, thought Katrina. The woman had been so helpful when she was dealing with her own gender-based discrimination case in the department, but when it came to standing up to racism, the woman was a grade-A chicken.

Katrina interlaced her fingers behind her head. "I still don't understand what this has to do with me. If you think someone leaked the information, then you'd better dissolve the whole committee—though it's a ludicrous step—but it's the only option if you are hell-bent on persecuting us. Besides, what difference does it make? It's not as if telling him is going to change the results. Quincy doesn't have any influence on the process and this whole cloak-and-dagger charade of the tenure game in the twenty-first century is ridiculous. Why shouldn't he know? He has to work with these people every day."

She paused and took a bite of her maple bar. "And I certainly want to know who has my back and who is ready to stab it."

Dean Bullard blinked. He cleared his throat. "All well and good, Katrina, but there are rules. Rules we have to follow."

Yeah, when it's convenient for you to follow them, she thought.

"Did you tell Quincy Knight about the tenure result?"

"No."

"Have you told him anything about the process?"

"He came to my office in tears. I gave him a hug and told him it would be alright. Perhaps he interpreted my hug in a particular way. We're friends. That's what friends do—comfort each other. You know, like human beings?"

"Well, that's exactly why you're here. You're the closest to him. Probably the only one who is friends with him on the committee."

"For fuck's sake."

"I'd appreciate it if you'd didn't swear in our meetings."

Abso-fucking-lutely, Dean Bullard. "As you wish." She sighed. "So what now? Why the urgency this morning? Are we going to drag this out for months like some other useless university committee?"

His mouth puckered and then relaxed. Puckered and then relaxed. She had noticed he did this when he was particularly upset. It was one of the few signs in his bovine personality that indicated there was blood in his veins. "I'm afraid these accusations are so serious I'll have to suspend you and put you on administrative leave."

Katrina's heart leapt into her throat. "Administrative leave? You mean like when a cop murders someone and the police force doesn't know what to do?"

He shook his head and sighed. "No, that's not why the police force puts officers on administrative leave. It gives them time to investigate the matter."

"So you're basically saying that comforting a friend who is going through an utterly useless arcane process—and a racist one at that—is equivalent to shooting someone."

"There's no need to raise your voice."

Katrina slammed her fist on the table and stood up. Coffee from the dean's mug splashed all over the gleaming oval table.

"I'll gladly be on suspension from this circus. And I'll certainly be relieved not to see the face of the head clown."

She scooped up the remainder of her maple bar and marched out the door. And slammed it so hard the dean's certificate of appreciation on the door fell to the floor and shattered with a satisfying tinkling of glass.

15

"I brought the bread, cheese, and wine. Sorry, no pirate's rum this time. I'm fresh out." Katrina held up a baguette in one hand and wine bottle in another.

"What happened?" Adi peered at Katrina with concern. "Your face is all red. Have you been crying?"

Katrina let her bag, wine, and baguette fall onto the table. She slumped into a chair and told Adi about her morning encounter with the dean.

Adi burst out laughing.

"It's not funny. I'm suspended."

Wiping away their tears, Adi said, "But I've never heard of a professor being suspended. At least not for something like this. Only for being a sex offender."

"Yeah, well, welcome to my world."

An intercom buzzed and Adi padded across the beige carpet to the door.

Katrina surveyed Adi's apartment. This was her first time there, and despite the fact it was in a block of soulless apartment buildings on the edge of the downtown, it felt cozy. Adi had decorated it with Christmas lights, comfortable shabby furniture, and a fake fireplace in the corner with their cat, Furbaby, curled up in a ball in a basket in front of it.

Zeynep floated into the kitchen, followed by Tala and Tamika.

"Tala! What happened to your eye?"

She giggled and pulled up the eyepatch. "It's fake, Professor Frost. Just a joke."

Katrina put a hand over her heart. "Sorry, I'm usually not so slow. It's been another day from hell. And you must really start to call me Katrina if we're going to be pirates together."

"It's hard to call you and Professor Scott by your first names. I want to be respectful."

Tamika slid onto a barstool and laughed. "I wish all our students were like you."

They stood in silence for a moment, listening to the cork pop of the wine and the glugging of the red liquid into glasses.

Zeynep held up a finger. "Only a glass per person. We need to be on our toes."

Katrina waved her glass. "About that, Zeynep. I'm afraid I've screwed up our plans for this evening. I won't be able to go."

Tamika's eyes widened. "It's about Quincy, isn't it. And rank and tenure."

"How did you know?" asked Katrina.

"Blipton is a small town within a small town. The grapevine is tightly packed."

"C'mon. Let me play host." Adi slammed the fridge door shut and carried a cutting board with bread, cheese, and dried fruit into the small living room.

Tala lowered herself into a fuzzy green chair that looked like it might swallow her up. "Professor Scott—I mean, Tamika—is right. I even heard about what happened. Though I don't know anything about tenure. The students all know you've been suspended."

Katrina sighed. "Yes, I can see how crazy it looks to an outsider. Because it is crazy. Being on the rank and tenure committee—there's one at the college level and one at the university level—is equivalent to being on a jury in a murder trial. It's that serious. If anyone finds out about the results or anything going on in the committee, the university will come down on you like a ton of bricks. Because I'm the only one who's friends with one of the people coming up for tenure, they assumed the so-called leak came from me. And I'll admit that I told him everything was going to be fine, which was interpreted as telling him the outcome of the vote. I can see why they'd think that, but what's so ridiculous is he'll find out the outcome one way or another in a few months' time."

Zeynep rubbed Katrina's shoulder. "Don't worry, Katrina. You know you'll come out a hero eventually."

"Eventually when I'm dead," she said sulkily. Then she lifted her head and smiled. "But I'm going to be positive, right?"

Katrina's phone buzzed. "Speak of the devil." She wandered into the back bedroom and braced herself for whatever Quincy had to say.

"Katrina!" he began. "I'm so sorry. Let me explain."

"Go on, I'm listening. Though I'm not sure they haven't tapped our phones."

"You know how much my department hates me. I had a mini breakdown after our last department meeting. Everyone glared at me. I swear I went to Cheryl's office just to vent about the department, since it's her job to deal with departmental problems. She's a good listener."

"And you broke down and told her about our conversation."

Quincy sniffed and blew his nose. His voice quavered. "I said something about how I knew everything would be alright, but that I just kept worrying that my department wouldn't support me. Cheryl, damn her, picked up on the first part."

"And then you said, 'Katrina told me.'"

"No! I swear I didn't. I just said that I'd heard through the grapevine everything would be alright. She pushed me on it and I didn't say anything."

"You're sure you didn't mention my name."

"I may be an idiot, but I didn't go that far. A day later, Bullard called me and said they were investigating a serious breach of confidentiality on the committee. He asked me point-blank if you were the one who told me and I said absolutely not. Then Cheryl kept leaving similar voicemails."

Katrina groaned.

"Katrina, I'm so sorry. I won't ask you to forgive me now because I'm sure you want to kill me. But please understand I won't do anything to jeopardize your position, no matter what."

"I get it, Quincy. That's why I comforted you when you were in tears in my office. The six years leading up to tenure is enough to make anyone crack. I just don't understand why they are obsessed with protecting an outcome that will be obvious to you in a few months anyway." She paused. "I've got to go. But thanks for calling. You're right that I can't forgive you right now, but I appreciate you telling me what happened and also not bringing my name into it. As long as we both keep quiet, they can't do anything."

"Thanks, Katrina. I owe you."

"You bet you do! Take care."

Katrina padded out into the living room. "That was the tenure candidate. I won't repeat his name in case Adi's apartment is bugged. I feel a little better, but not much. I need a distraction."

Rubbing her forefinger and thumb together, Zeynep murmured agreement. She stared into space.

"You look like you want to tell us tonight's plan. Finally," said Tamika.

"What? Oh yes. Let's see." She carefully placed her wineglass on the table and stood up. "If we're going to put pressure on the administration, first we need to find a lever. If we give them what they want, then they'll have to give us what we want, right?"

"If we play our cards right," murmured Katrina.

Zeynep nodded. "You all know the university is forever in search of money. Especially these days. The problem is that donors are few and far between in Snake's Canyon. So Blipton needs to rely on donors from the outside."

"You mean from larger cities?" asked Tala.

"That too. What I mean is they need sources of money unconnected to living in Snake's Canyon."

"Such as parents and alumni?" asked Tamika.

"Exactly. And not just any parents and alumni, but rich ones. And rich ones who will donate."

Tamika sighed. "Always the same story, isn't it."

"We'll use it to our advantage this time. The university can't figure out how to admit the richest students because of its needs-blind policy. And its supposed social justice mission statement says it doesn't give preferential treatment to rich people, particularly rich white people given the way generational wealth works in this country."

"Wait a minute," said Tamika. "The university is always moaning about its budget, but it finds plenty of money to pay administrators and keep expanding with new buildings every year. Every year they say there'll be budget cuts, but they almost never materialize. The faculty and staff don't get raises, students and parents pay more, but they keep crying wolf."

"That's why this isn't only about trying to fund the university. It's about greed. And about shady dealings like the ones you told me your nephew uncovered, Tamika," said Zeynep.

Tamika took another sip of wine and grimaced.

Zeynep continued. "The other thing the university is constantly worried about is security. Specifically quelling student disturbances like the sit-in last year."

Katrina snorted. "Yep. Freedom of speech looks good on paper, but they're not so enthusiastic when it's directed at them."

"But how on earth can we help with security?" asked Tala. "I thought you were talking about money. We can't promise to police the campus."

"No," said Zeynep. "But it's a case of two birds—the funds, the security, all in one package. We'll promise to give them what they want. But it will be a fake. We will con them."

"Yes!" cried Katrina. She and Tamika clinked glasses.

"Shhh...you two. I'm trying to listen," chided Adi.

"I'm not sure everyone knows this, but Tala is not a rising star in the computer science department—"

"Even though my parents wanted me to go into nursing." Tala lifted her triangular chin. "And the only woman of color in my class."

Everyone clapped and hooted.

Zeynep smiled. "Tala is at the top of her class. And a computer genius."

Tala sank back into the folds of the fuzzy green chair.

"Oh, c'mon, don't be modest," said Adi.

"She's well known among her professors as a whiz at creating algorithms to get particular outcomes. Like online stores use to tell you what to buy next based on what you bought before. Ideally, we'd have Tala offer to sell an algorithm to a trustee. Or maybe more than one trustee. To do that, we'll need an introduction, and I think softening up Dean Bullard is the best way."

"But what kind of algorithm?" asked Adi.

"One they can use for the admissions process. This algorithm will guarantee the highest-paying students and by proxy the highest-paying parents. And, because they still need to admit middle-class and lower-income students, the algorithm will select those students who have the most compliant backgrounds."

"The ones who will be too afraid or too complacent to protest or cause bad publicity for the university?" asked Katrina.

"Exactly." Zeynep's thin frame was quivering with excitement.

"You mean Tala has created such an algorithm? Why would we want to give such an algorithm to the university? To make it more of a hellhole than it already is?" asked Katrina.

"Sweet, innocent history professor Frost," said Tamika. "I've studied algorithms as an economics professor, but I have no idea how you'd create one like that. My guess is we'll sell them a lemon, won't we, Zeynep?"

She nodded. "We're selling them a promise. They'll pay us and then we have something on them, too."

"Wait." Adi swallowed a dried apple ring. "We sell them a fake admissions formula. They pay us a ton of money. And then what? What happens when they find out the formula is a fake?"

Tala cleared her throat. "I've already designed a perfectly plausible formula. It's just incorrect. It will do nothing to the admissions pool."

"But what happens when they find out it's a fake?" asked Katrina.

"First of all, they may or may not find out. They may believe there aren't as many wealthy students as they had hoped, but they have no way of testing whether those students are conformists or not. Second, even if they do smell a rat, what are they going to do? Come after us? We'd expose them."

"How?" Tamika propped up her head with her arm on the couch.

"We'll have recordings of them agreeing to do the deal. We'd expose them. Not only would they be off the board, but their other financial interests would be hurt. Not to mention their reputations."

"How does this help us get revenge? Other than taking their money?" asked Katrina.

"I have a plan for the money. Some of it will go to us, but the rest will go to a good cause. Trust me. It's better if you don't know about it right now so you don't give anything away."

Katrina fluttered her eyelids and put a dainty hand on her heart. "I am the soul of discretion."

Tamika burst out laughing. Everyone followed. Soon Katrina joined in.

When the giggling had died down, Katrina said, "But what about Tala's parents? And Deans Bullard and Hackett? And Batu? And Adi's job? And Tamika's nephew?"

Tamika gave Katrina a gentle punch in the upper arm. "Zeynep may be a pirate magician, but that's all a tall order."

A ghost of a smile flickered across Zeynep's lips. "Don't be too sure. I've got a few rabbits up my sleeve."

16

The intercom buzzed. Then Tamika's phone buzzed.

Everyone fell silent.

Adi marched to the door as if they were ready to tell off a persistent solicitor.

Tamika scanned her phone and then yelled in Adi's direction. "It'll be my nephew. Can you let him in?"

"How did Gabriel know where you are? And why is he here?" asked Katrina.

Tamika drained her glass of wine. "I told him everywhere I'd be today, in case there was a problem. You must have seen the newspaper ran the story he asked them to withhold."

As Tamika greeted a tearful Gabriel, Katrina filled in the crew about Gabriel's story.

He hugged everyone. He had an angelic smile, but his sunken eyes darted warily around the room.

He opened his mouth to speak but Adi interrupted him. "You'll stay here as long as you need to, okay? Make yourself at home. I have a spare bedroom, mostly occupied by my cat, but she'll have to make peace with you as a roommate or else she can move in with me." Adi waved Gabriel toward the back bedroom.

Tala leaned in and whispered, "Why is he here and not at your house, Professor Scott?"

"The dean and his merry band of gangsters will be searching for him at my house. They'd never think to try Adi's place."

Zeynep glanced at her watch. "We'd better get ready for the gala. Tamika and Tala brought their own fancy gear." She looked at Katrina. "What about you?"

"I haven't a stitch to wear, fairy godmother!"

Tamika peered at her doubtfully. "I brought another dress, but I doubt we're the same size."

Katrina waved her hand. "It doesn't matter anyway, remember? I'm suspended. There's no way I can be a guest at the gala now."

"I've made a plan," said Zeynep. "We'll have to sneak you in. Undercover."

TAMIKA AND TALA waltzed into the living room. Tamika wore a figure-hugging scarlet velvet gown with a shallow open V-neck. Tala wore a floaty black dress with tiny pink and blue flowers. By contrast, Zeynep and Adi looked like undertakers in their black university catering uniforms. Adi added flair by twisting the collar and pushing up the sleeves.

Zeynep held up a campus security uniform with a black baseball cap.

"Are you kidding me? Campus security? Me?" asked Katrina.

"Don't forget the time you knocked out that guy who was harassing Tamika last year," said Zeynep.

"It's true," said Tamika. "You might have been a bouncer if you hadn't become a professor."

Katrina's eyes narrowed. "What are you trying to say? I'm built like a bouncer?"

"I wish I were built like a bouncer," sighed Adi. "It's a compliment, Katrina."

"Backhanded. Or underhanded."

Zeynep ran into the kitchen and returned a split second later. "Here. Eat this. Now. I order you." She handed Katrina a gold-foil-wrapped chocolate bar.

"Zuster chocolate? Where did you get this? It's my absolute favorite!" Katrina tore through the foil, snapped off a piece and popped it into her mouth. She smiled and offered the others the bar, only with slight hesitation.

"We have to keep an eye on Katrina. She gets hangry," said Zeynep.

"It's called hypoglycemia. It's a medical condition," snapped Katrina in between bites. Her shoulders relaxed. "Sorry. But it is chemical. Really."

Zeynep gave her a reassuring pat on her shoulder. "That's why I have a stash of chocolate at work."

"I appreciate it. Back to my security guard role—won't they recognize me?" Katrina held up the uniform and grimaced.

"Not with the baseball cap they won't. Besides, people see what they expect to see," said Tala. She held up an earpiece. "And we have this handy earpiece so you can communicate with all of us."

Katrina bit into another piece of the chocolate. "It's a good thing this uniform doesn't have any weapons attached."

"Why?" asked Tamika.

"Because I'd be too tempted to use them on Dean Hackett."

17

———

"Remember, everyone has a role. Only one glass of champagne. Keep in contact at all times." They all stood in a circle in the grass at the back of Felton Hall, a lovely Georgian building used to entertain alumni. Caterers hurried back and forth past them in an ant-like stream.

"How do we communicate with you, Katrina? We all have our phones so we can text or call, but you can't," said Tamika.

"Tala rigged it so Katrina and I can have conversations with our two earpieces," said Zeynep. "Then I can communicate to all of you."

"Can't I just text you all?" asked Katrina.

"You can try, but you'll draw attention to yourself. Security is strict about not using your phone while you're on duty at an event," said Zeynep. "A friend was fired for texting his girlfriend while he was working an event."

Tamika shifted on her tall green heels, but they still kept sinking into the soft earth. "So how's this going to work?"

"Adi and I will circulate with trays of food. We'll try to redirect people toward you," said Zeynep. "Don't look so sour, Katrina."

Katrina realized her bottom lip jutted up over her top lip. "Sorry. Maybe it's better if I sit this one out."

Tamika put a hand on Katrina's shoulder. "You know you're acting like a spoiled child who is used to getting her way."

Everyone inhaled and held their breath.

Katrina's shoulders slumped. "You're right. I suppose I'm tired." She waved her hand around the circle. "I apologize, everyone. I'm short on sleep, still pretty shaken from the car crash, and worried in general. Though it's no excuse to snap at you. Please, do go on."

Zeynep smiled. "You'll be in the best position to view the crowd. If someone arrives or leaves, you can tell me through your radio. You can also direct Adi and I to the right spot."

"Got it."

"Adi!"

The circle parted as another member of the catering staff bounced toward them, grinning.

Zeynep leaned over and whispered to Katrina, "Whoever that is, they're in love with Adi. What a ridiculous grin."

Katrina chuckled and nodded.

"I didn't know you were on the catering staff!" cried the bouncy one.

Adi smiled back but then looked alarmed as her friend pulled her away from the circle.

"I suppose it's our cue," said Tamika. "And good thing, too. This mud out here is like quicksand."

"True. But I bet it's nothing like the quicksand we're about to walk into," muttered Katrina.

———

Pulling down her baseball cap, Katrina marched after Tamika and Tala, doing her best impression of a clomping security guard. The boots weighed at least a hundred pounds, so it was relatively easy. Though it was difficult to keep up with Tamika and Tala's light steps. Katrina pulled out a square of toilet paper she had taken from the bathroom and wiped her brow. It wasn't hot inside, but it was humid.

Then, as if a DJ had turned up the volume, the chatter in the room increased, echoing across the high ceiling. Katrina pressed her earpiece deeper in her ear. She couldn't hear anything. This was such a stupid plan. They'd never be able to accomplish anything this way.

A hand grasped her arm.

Her whole body tensed—she knew she couldn't get away with this disguise.

"Hey—we need an officer by the microphone. Now."

Katrina nodded without glancing back and let out a burst of air. Thank God he thought she was legit. But where was the fucking microphone? Then the sharp sound of a microphone test going wrong filled the air.

"What are you waiting for?"

Katrina stumbled toward the mic, looking for any nearby reason to avoid the stage. She spotted a tall, thin man with oddly fashionable Coke-bottle glasses. Patrick what's-his-face—a trustee. Katrina clomped toward him, veering at the last second and bumping into a waiter with a tray. Glasses fell onto Patrick's tailored suit, splattering it with a mixture of red and white wine.

Pulling her baseball cap firmly over her eyes, she headed off at top speed, then glanced back. A small crowd had formed behind her. The waiter waved her arms and pointed at Katrina.

Katrina weaved through the crowd, as fast as her leaden legs would go.

She'd hide in the women's bathroom. A perfect place to disappear.

Fuck. A line snaked out of the women's bathroom.

She ducked into the men's bathroom and made a beeline for a stall. Once inside, she took off her hat and slumped against the doorway.

The men's room was blessedly silent.

Then she heard streaming liquid. And it wasn't the water faucet.

"Patrick. Looks like you've had an accident."

Now the faucet had been turned on.

"A stupid security guard bumped into me."

The other voice sounded familiar.

"I want to talk to you about someone. Might as well since no one else is here."

It was Dean Hackett.

"Yeah? Who?"

Katrina was distracted by the noise from her earpiece.

"Katrina. Are you there?"

She pulled out the earpiece. There was no way she could respond to Zeynep, so she might as well listen in on the conversation.

"She's been a lot of trouble lately," said Hackett.

Dammit. She had missed who they were talking about.

"Funny you should say that. I heard about her from Shane Bivens today—Dean Bullard told him he put her on administrative leave. Sounds like she really screwed up rank and tenure, but I don't understand why Bivens hates her so much. Did he make a pass and she rejected him?"

Katrina gulped and backed away from the door, nearly tripping over the toilet seat.

"Well, she threatened me yesterday," said Hackett.

"About what?" asked Bullard.

"Doesn't matter. The point is we need to get rid of her. And fast."

18

———

Katrina inhaled the fresh air and wriggled her nose at the smell of mud—or was it fresh fertilizer? She leaned against the tree trunk near the entrance to the gala. Her queasiness began to disappear.

So Bullard and Hackett were after her. It wasn't her imagination. She'd need to tell the others, though she knew they had to focus on their mission.

"Katrina! Where are you? We need you!" screeched the earpiece dangling from her neck.

She inserted it back into her ear. "Sorry. I had to catch my breath outside. It's a long story, but I found out Bullard and Hackett are plotting against me."

Silence.

"Are you there, Zeynep?"

"Are you surprised?" asked Zeynep.

"No I'm not fucking surprised!"

She heard a squawk and looked up. A scandalized mother clapped her hands over her child's ears. The child grinned deviously.

Katrina held up a placating hand. "Sorry. Sorry."

She hissed in the earpiece. "Thanks for the sympathy, Zeynep."

"Sorry, Katrina. I didn't mean to be short with you, but we've got a situation brewing in here and we need your help."

"Okay. Where should I go?"

"Tamika and Tala haven't been able to get hold of Bullard, the snake. He keeps slithering away from them. But they're on the case. They're talking to Sally Spriggs from the Center for Community Interfacing right now, so I need you to get close enough to record the conversation."

"I thought Tamika and Tala had their phones. Can't they record her?"

"It's way too noisy in here. Besides, Tamika's battery ran out. I gave you the most powerful recorder we have. You don't have to get too close."

"Okay. Where are they at?"

"Near the desserts."

"Excellent."

"And one more thing, Katrina."

"Yes?"

"Don't get distracted by the chocolate cake."

"Wouldn't dream of it."

Luckily, the dessert table, laden with luscious cakes and pies, was near the entrance. So, too, were Tala, Tamika, and Sally.

Katrina switched on the recorder and crossed her arms, as if she were the dessert guard.

Sally Spriggs was a washed-out blonde white woman in her late forties. The kind who smiled and nodded but was hard as ice underneath. Katrina was comfortable with her because they were so similar. They'd both stop at nothing to achieve their goals. The difference was they had radically different goals.

Sally's tennis bracelet made a soft whipping noise as she waved a hand. "Yes. It's Aragon Partners who are the developers for the dorms."

"I read that in the paper today. Quite a surprising story."

Sally looked knowing. "I wouldn't be surprised if there were a few resignations in the near future."

"This kind of corruption makes me mad," said Tala.

"And it reflects so poorly on the university," said Tamika.

"You can say that again," Sally waved her wineglass. "Look—here's Dean Bullard."

Bullard trundled into the small circle. "Sally! It's been ages. How are things over at the center?"

"Just fine, just fine." She looked at her phone. "Excuse me, I said I'd meet someone and I'm late." Sally scurried away.

Odd, thought Katrina. Why was she in such a hurry to leave the charming company of Dean Bullard?

Bullard cleared his throat. "I'm sorry we didn't get a chance to finish our intriguing conversation, Professor Scott and Tala. Please do go on."

"Well, as I said before, the admissions office pulled me in—confidentially, of course—to help with enrollment projections in the fall. Not surprisingly, it was wrong. Yet again."

Bullard paused.

"Oh, don't worry, Dean Bullard. Tala is a part of this conversation for a reason."

"I see. Do go on."

"Tala was in my advanced economics class. And I used the example of admission rates as a difficult issue of projection—not specific to Blipton University, you understand. Tala here, star student that she is, came up with a brilliant solution."

Tala's ponytail swayed back and forth. "You know what a computer algorithm is, right, Dean Bullard? It's like a program that recognizes patterns of behavior. When you shop online, an algorithm tries to sell you the stuff it thinks you're likely to buy next."

He nodded. "Of course."

"I developed an algorithm the admissions office can use to process applications. They already use a basic one to sort through the applications. But this algorithm would be more advanced," said Tala.

Tamika lowered her voice. "This algorithm would select students who can pay full tuition. And their parents, by logical extension, would also be likely to donate."

Tala choked on her punch. She coughed and coughed. "Excuse me..." She waved her hand and moved away. As she brushed past Katrina, she whispered, "Watch this."

Tamika lightly touched Bullard's lower arm. They were about level in height as Tamika was wearing her heels. She leaned in. "Tala's work was brilliant. And I tweaked the algorithm to produce one more result."

Katrina's stomach turned as she listened to Bullard's heavy breathing.

"The extra result was to find students who are likely to be compliant. No troublemakers. Understand?"

His head nodded slowly. Katrina knew his brain wasn't quick enough to process this complex information.

"So this formula—I mean, algorithm—can guarantee rich students and students who won't make trouble?"

"You've got it."

"But aren't you against that politically? And why are you telling me?"

Katrina had to admit he was more savvy than she realized.

"It's a reality that this school needs rich students to keep its administrative expansion going. I'd like to be a dean one day myself. And as far as compliance goes, remember I'm in economics—a conservative field in all senses of the word."

Silence.

Tamika licked her lips. "And if you think all Black people are revolutionaries, or people ready to go into the streets, well, you'd better check your stereotypes."

Katrina grinned.

"Oh, no-no-no-no...I'd never..." Bullard blubbered.

Tamika smiled. "And as for why I'm telling you—well, that's a little more complex. I imagine the trustees would be willing to offer a generous donation in exchange, don't you?"

"Why would they give a donation?"

Tamika sighed. "Because our trustees are so wealthy they're after connections and power, rather than money. If we can make them look good because they helped turn around the university after years of budget crises, I bet they'd be willing to pay."

Bullard looked shifty. "I wouldn't be too sure. Who gets the money?"

"Well...Tala needs to pay off her hundred thousand dollars in student loans. I also have fifty thousand in loans. And we'd both need extra funds, because, you understand, we could sell this for more to another university. But we're both loyal to Blipton."

"Right, right. To be frank, I'm not exactly in a position to approach the trustees at this time. There have been...conflicts...in the past. But I'll see what I can do."

"What do you mean by that, exactly?"

"Oh, I, ah...aside from the trustees, there are certain individuals, local businesspeople, who have made very generous donations to Blipton in the past, people who I'm in close contact with. There's a chance that one of them might be persuaded to contribute. Purely with a view to safeguarding the best interests of the university, of course," he added hastily. "I'll approach him about it. Ask what he thinks. I'll get back to you soon."

Tala came springing back up. "Sorry I had to leave. What did I miss?"

19

———

The leftover apple pie Katrina had liberated from the gala slid out of its box and onto the doormat. She moaned. "Why did you stop so suddenly?"

"Shhhh!" Adi held up one finger.

The door to Adi's apartment stood ajar.

"What is it?" hissed Tamika from behind Katrina.

Adi's head twisted back and forward. They grabbed a large umbrella next to the door.

"Here. Give this to Adi," hissed Tala. She handed Katrina a large folding knife. Katrina goggled at the size of it.

"I'm a woodcarver in my spare time," she hissed.

With equally wide eyes, Adi took the knife and flipped open the blade.

They all slipped off their shoes.

With high, slow steps, they filed into the apartment behind Adi.

A soft glow came from the kitchen, so there was no need for a light.

Katrina sniffed. Perfume. Or aftershave? It smelled vaguely familiar.

Adi moved into the kitchen and Tala and Katrina crept into the hallway.

Tala held up a finger. Katrina stopped.

Breathing. She listened closely. It was more like wheezing.

Katrina and Tala stood behind the door to the bedroom. With an exaggerated motion, Katrina counted off with her fingers and pushed open the door.

Two yellow eyes peered at them in the darkness.

Tala clutched her chest. "It's Furbaby."

Katrina flipped the light switch. "But it's not just Furbaby. Look at this room!"

Adi, Tamika, and Zeynep rushed in. "Oh no!" Adi held their head in their hands. "It's as bad as the kitchen!"

Clothes were strewn everywhere, drawers had been pulled out of the dresser, and poor Furbaby was huddled on the floor. Katrina scooped her up and massaged the distressed cat's neck. Soon she began to purr and knead Katrina's unlovely uniform.

"Has anything been taken?" asked Zeynep.

Adi sat on the bed and stared at the clothes pile on the floor. "The TV and stereo are there, but they're not worth more than a few hundred dollars. I have some cash stowed in the kitchen, but they didn't find it."

Tamika put a hand on Adi's shoulder. "What about your laptop?"

Adi put a hand up to their mouth. "Shit. Shit. I didn't see it." Then they let out a sigh. "I left it at work. Whew."

"So what were they after?" asked Tala.

Before she had a chance to answer, Tamika gasped and ran from the room. They could hear her banging doors as she careened through the apartment.

"What is it?" Katrina called.

"I can't believe this," Tamika shouted back, "but in all the excitement I forgot!"

"Forgot what?" Zeynep looked slightly exasperated.

"Gabriel! Where's Gabriel?"

———

THE PIRATE QUEENS sat in a small, tight circle in Adi's living room. Even the Christmas lights were askew. At least Furbaby made the gathering less gloomy. Katrina had never heard a cat purr so loudly.

Adi ambled into the kitchen.

Zeynep rubbed her forefinger and thumb in a circular motion. "I know this is a stupid question, Tamika, but did you check for a text from Gabriel?"

Tamika shook her head. "My phone stopped working at the party, remember?"

"Oh. You're right. I completely forgot. My charger is on the desk if that helps?"

In two steps Tamika was at the desk, but her face fell as she jabbed the charger cable against her phone. "It's the wrong kind."

"Does anyone else have Gabriel's number? Do you remember the number, Tamika?"

She shook her head. "You know how it is—there's no need to remember anyone's number anymore. I barely remember my own."

"What's that sound? Is it hail?" asked Katrina. "Is the apocalypse coming?"

"It's popcorn, silly!" yelled Adi from the kitchen. "I'm making it the old-fashioned way. You know, in a pot!"

The warm, earthy smell floated into the living room. Katrina's stomach rumbled.

"Is there any other way we can get in touch with Gabriel?" asked Tala.

"I suppose Adi could search his student record, but their computer is at school," said Zeynep, ever the practical one. She bit her lip. "Tamika, you don't suppose..."

Tamika bounced up and leaned over Zeynep. "I know what you're thinking. I know what you're all thinking."

"No, no. I don't mean that."

Adi padded in with a tray laden with popcorn, red wine, and a pitcher of water. "This should cheer us up. What did I miss?"

Tala intervened. "We were discussing what might have happened to Gabriel." She held out her hand for the lifeless phone.

Tamika paced back and forth in her stockinged feet. "Zeynep was about to accuse Gabriel of being a thief, weren't you?"

"No, no, Tamika. I promise. What I was about to say was I wonder if Gabriel escaped. I noticed there was a fire escape in the bedroom. Perhaps he heard the intruder and left the building. He's probably been trying to call you but can't get through for obvious reasons."

Tamika flopped down on the couch. "I'm sorry I doubted you. It's just, well, you know."

They all nodded their heads.

"The good news is he probably hasn't gone too far. He's probably wandering around outside, waiting for us to come home," said Zeynep.

"Then where is he? We've been home for at least thirty minutes," said Katrina.

Zeynep shot her a warning glance.

Katrina responded by munching on popcorn.

"Professor Scott—I mean, Tamika—would you give me your phone?" Tala said. "Maybe I can fix it."

"Oh, honey. Would you? Here you go."

"I thought of another problem. Though it's obviously less important than Gabriel. How is Dean Bullard going to get in touch with Tamika about the algorithm if he can't talk to her?" asked Katrina.

"Good question. None of us can really contact him on your behalf because it would mess up the plan. I suppose Tala could, but that might appear odd," said Zeynep.

Tala held up the phone. "Problem solved! You just needed the right adapter."

"Bless you, child." Tamika grabbed Tala's arm as she frantically scrolled through her messages.

She looked up. "Gabriel is safe."

20

———

Tamika grabbed her red trench coat. Her arm struggled in the sleeve.

"Here, let me help." Katrina held the coat open. "Are you going to tell us where Gabriel is?"

"It's better if I go alone."

Katrina snorted. "Famous last words. Not a chance, *sweetie*."

Despite her distress, Tamika gave her the side eye.

Adi stood up and adjusted their thick 1960s glasses.

"Since when have you worn glasses?" Katrina asked.

"Doctor's orders. I must be getting old."

"Thirty is hardly old, Adi," said Zeynep. "I'm thirty-five." She tucked her hair behind her ear. "Sorry. I lost focus. Katrina's right— we'll go with you, Tamika."

Shaking her head, Tamika tightened the belt on her trench. "As much as I love you all, I can't take the four of you along. We'd be too obvious."

"Then why don't we split up and go separately?" asked Zeynep. "Where are we going, by the way?"

"You'll never believe it—Gabriel is at Sally Spriggs's house."

"Who? That woman from the Center for Community Interfacing? I didn't know they were that friendly."

"They're not," said Tamika. "Believe it or not, she was the burglar! He followed her home after she broke in."

Katrina chuckled. "Well, well. I had Sally down as a slightly flighty yes-woman. Guess there's more there than meets the eye."

"What was she doing in my apartment?" Adi demanded.

Tala flew out of her seat. "Let's find out! She's been so mean to me in the past. I'd like to get some dirt on her."

"You are a vengeful one, aren't you?" asked an amused Katrina.

Tala's shoulders sagged.

"Pirate queens!" Zeynep clapped her hands. "Time to focus. We'll take two cars to Sally's house. Does she live in a house, Tamika?"

"Yes. At 1654 Sycamore. It's in the hills. Most of those houses have large yards, front and back."

"So let's drive by and pick up Gabriel." Adi jiggled their leg.

Tamika held up a finger. "There's one thing I didn't mention. Gabriel is inside the house. Somehow he got inside—I'm not clear from his text about how it happened."

Tala gasped. "But how will we get him out?"

Furbaby was being given such an intense neck massage by Zeynep that she slid off the couch, presumably to escape. "We'll play it by ear. We may need to go inside to get him out. Perhaps Tamika can distract Sally and then he'll escape."

Katrina rolled down the window and inhaled the humid night air as they rolled up to 1654 Sycamore. Or, rather just before it. The brakes on Adi's ancient Corolla squeaked as they came to a halt. They had decided it was better to go in one car since two would be more noticeable.

"Time for a new car, Adi," said Katrina.

"Sorry. I didn't hear you, backseat driver."

"Aha! Adi has a sarcastic streak after all," said Katrina.

"It only comes out during times of extreme stress," sighed Adi.

"Don't worry, Adi. We'll be able to go to sleep soon. Zeynep has a plan." Tala looked at Zeynep. "Don't you?"

Zeynep gave her a wan smile. "I wish I did."

Adi sighed.

Tamika opened the door and held up a turquoise silk scarf. "Well, I'm ready to go. I'm going to tell Sally she left behind this beautiful scarf at the party."

"How did you get it and why are you bringing it this late at night?"

"It was by accident. After she left, I saw the scarf hanging next to my coat." She paused and pointed at the house. "See how the lights are on in her front room? I'll tell her I'd planned to leave it on her doorstep but as the lights were on, I thought I'd ring the bell."

"I don't know..." Adi trailed off. "What if she has a gun and thinks you're an intruder?"

"You always think of the worst-case scenario, don't you?" Tamika took out her phone and dialed a number.

"How do you have her number?" asked Katrina.

"Got it at the party," hissed Tamika. She held up a hand. "Ah, yes, Sally? Sorry to bother you so late, but I have your scarf. Yes, your beautiful silk scarf. I was on my way home and thought I'd drop it by. Your lights are on, which is why I called. I didn't want to alarm you by showing up on your doorstep." She paused. "Great. I'll be up in a sec."

"I don't understand," said Tala. "How can we help Gabriel escape?"

Tamika leaned back. "He's locked in the office upstairs."

"Okay," said Katrina. "W-T-F? How did he manage to lock himself in?"

"He's a talented young man," sighed Tamika. "I'll distract Sally in the front part of the house. Meanwhile, you all can go through the back door. He said he slipped in through the sliding doors, so they should still be open."

"How will we find the office?" asked Zeynep.

"He said it's the first door on the left as you come up the stairs."

"We shouldn't all go," said Zeynep. "I nominate Katrina and Tala."

"Fine by me," said Adi. "Just hearing the plan makes me break out in hives."

"Why Katrina and Tala?" asked Tamika.

"Power and grace," said Zeynep.

"Oh, thanks a lot," grumbled Katrina.

"I mean you're the tallest among us—" said Zeynep.

"And cleverest," put in Tala.

"Excellent ass-kissing skills, Tala." Katrina smiled. "Let's go."

Tamika ambled slowly up the winding stone-covered pathway. Katrina and Tala slipped around the corner of the house, along a high hedge and into the backyard.

Tala grabbed Katrina's shoulder. "Wait!" she whispered.

Katrina froze. All she heard was a lonely cricket. Then she glimpsed a pinpoint of light. A red glow. Someone was smoking on the back patio. They crouched down behind the hedge. Katrina bent over as far as possible, even though the top of her head surely must be sticking out.

She heard the scraping of a metal on stone and then a smoker's cough. Shit. Whoever it was must be sitting on a chair, and that meant he wouldn't be moving soon. Katrina looked at Tala. Tala pointed at the next length of hedge running parallel to the back of the house. She made a walking gesture with her two fingers. Katrina nodded and followed her, still crouching down.

They arrived near the sliding glass doors. The smoker was directly in front of the doors. He was a short, squat man with a mullet-like haircut, sitting with one arm folded over his paunch, a leprechaun guarding his pot of gold.

Tala jabbed her finger straight ahead. Katrina shrugged and followed her around the back to a flimsy-looking door. Katrina had a hunch it led into the garage rather than the house, but it was worth a try. She jiggled the handle. Nothing.

She threw up her hands. Tala pulled a small screwdriver out of her back pocket. Katrina pantomimed awe with wide eyes and a grin. Back in her early days, she'd had some experience with minor breaking and entering. Her boyfriend had shown her how to break into people's backyards so they could swim in their pools at night. Of course, they had checked to make sure the homeowners had been on vacation.

Katrina jammed the screwdriver into the lock.

At first, she thought the scraping noise she heard was the lock breaking.

"Hurry!" hissed Tala. "He's getting up from the chair."

"Don't rush me. Besides, he'll go in through the sliding doors, won't he?"

"Sounds like he's coming toward us."

Katrina scrunched up her face and made one final twist of the screwdriver. The door burst open and the pair scurried inside.

"Hey!" a muffled voice yelled beyond the door.

Another door stood ajar on the sidewall of the garage, which Katrina figured must lead into the house, though she couldn't see in. She pointed at it, but Tala shook her head and squeezed down behind a dark blue BMW parked in the garage. Fortunately for Katrina, a black Range Rover stood next to the BMW. She crouched down, face level with the rear bumper.

The shuffling footsteps of the leprechaun entered the garage. Katrina held her breath and glanced at Tala. She stuck her head between her legs.

The footsteps stopped in front of the Range Rover. Katrina was sure the man would be able to smell her sweating if he couldn't see or hear her breathing. The footsteps moved closer.

"Ney? Are you there? Did you hear something strange?" Sally.

"You bet I did."

"The door was open. Do you think they came in the house?"

"I heard something. But it was coming from the living room." Praise the Lord. It was Tamika.

"I'm not sure." The footsteps came closer.

"Well, I'm not going in there alone," said Sally. "C'mon, Ney."

"Alright. But I swear they came in here."

"Hurry!" hissed Sally.

Footsteps retreated into the house.

With a sigh, Katrina looked at Tala. They both nodded. Tala leapt up and sprang lightly across the garage to the door. Katrina winced as she straightened up and walked over stiffly.

Tala waved her hand impatiently. Katrina stumbled through the open doorway after her, into the darkness.

21

Katrina's fingertips skimmed the rough surface. Then the wall became smooth. She couldn't see a thing, so she grabbed Tala's shoulder. She breathed the slightly stale wet-dog-on-a-carpet smell. Dog. Oh God, where was the dog?

Tala pointed a finger upward as her shoulder lifted. Stairs. Well, at least they were getting closer to Gabriel. Miraculously, they arrived at the summit. Weak light filtered in from an upstairs window. Then she heard a gentle snore. Katrina grabbed Tala's shoulder and motioned to her ear. Was someone else in the house, sleeping? Running through past conversations in her mind, Katrina remembered quite clearly that Sally lived alone, save an occasional boyfriend like this Ney character.

They turned to the left, as per their instructions. Katrina detected the source of the snoring. A small brown-and-white speckled dog sat curled in a basket at the end of the hallway. Some guard dog, she thought sourly.

Ignoring the dog, Tala held her face up to the first door on the left. "Gabriel?" she whispered.

"Yes," came the reply.

Katrina inserted the screwdriver in the doorknob. This time, the job was easier. The door popped open and Gabriel rushed out. The trio ran to the stairs. They froze. Chattering voices floated upward.

"We'd better check upstairs," said Ney.

Gabriel pointed to the door opposite them. They filed into the bathroom. Heavy footsteps came up the stairs. Katrina spun around wildly. It was a long, narrow pink-tiled bathroom with a sink, toilet, and tub. A small linen closet stood at the entry. Only Tala could fit in there. She did so, squeezing herself in between the toilet paper and towels.

"The shower curtain," said Gabriel. He leapt into the tub and pulled the pink shower curtain around the tub. Katrina got in as well and held the two pieces of the curtain shut.

The door opened. Katrina examined the shower curtain more closely, Though pink, it was not exactly opaque. Surely they were visible, as if they were the victims of the shower attack in *Psycho*.

Gabriel, whose face was already covered in a thick layer of sweat, stared dully at the curtain. A man resigned to his fate.

"Nothing in here!" yelled Tamika.

Thank you, sweet Jesus.

The footsteps retreated downstairs.

Tala and Gabriel nimbly left their hiding places, while Katrina found herself wound up in the shower curtain. After three tries, she finally extracted herself and rushed out of the bathroom.

Tala and Gabriel had disappeared. She looked across to Gabriel's hiding place. Nothing.

Then she peered over the bannister. Nothing. She slipped down the stairway into the darkness.

A hand grabbed her.

She spun around.

It was Gabriel. He held a finger to his lips and pointed to Tala. She tiptoed toward the garage door. Gabriel and Katrina followed and soon they were in the fresh night air. Katrina noticed an opening in the hedge and squeezed through it, waving along Tala and Gabriel. Half bent over, they ran single file down the perimeter of the front lawn to the sidewalk. They straightened up and walked casually toward the car.

The engine revved to life as the trio rushed into the back seat.

"Where's Tamika?" asked Zeynep.

Tamika half-walked, half-ran out of the front door.

Sally appeared at the doorway. She yelled, "Tamika! What do you think you're doing?"

Katrina's heart skipped and then thudded even more loudly than before.

Tamika turned around slowly on one heel.

"Yes?"

"The scarf!"

Tamika held a hand to her head and laughed. "I completely forgot about it in the commotion. You two better lock up. It's not safe these days with all sorts wandering about."

Katrina snorted.

Tamika ran lightly on her heels toward Sally with the turquoise scarf fluttering behind her. The instant it was handed over, she made her escape.

"Drive, dammit, drive!" she breathed as she tumbled into the back seat on top of Gabriel, Katrina, and Tala.

———

Katrina held up a limp fry, stared at it, and popped it into her mouth. Just what she needed. She held up another and wagged it at Zeynep. "Want one? They're hot and delicious."

Zeynep wrinkled her nose. "No, thanks. Not hungry. And even if I were..." She trailed off.

"You wouldn't dream of criticizing our food, would you?" asked Adi.

"Something like that." Zeynep tucked her hair behind her ear. "Tell us how you got out of there."

While Tala recounted their adventures, Katrina switched on her phone. Texts from her mom. She surveyed the crew, squeezed into a booth. They were the only customers at fatties burgers, save one man in a green bathrobe at the other end of the restaurant.

"Earth to Katrina. Are you there?" asked Tamika.

"Oh, sorry, I wasn't listening. What are we talking about?"

Tamika sighed. "Gabriel is telling his story."

Gabriel smiled. "As I was saying, Sally broke into Adi's maybe two hours after you all left for the gala. I hid in the bedroom. Then I left by the fire escape. I couldn't tell if she took anything, so I followed her when she left the building."

Tamika rubbed his head. "I'm glad you did, sweetie, but you shouldn't have."

"Oh, let him be," said Katrina. "He's a journalist, after all."

Tamika glared at her. "Sorry," said Katrina. "I should stay out of family matters, shouldn't I?" She paused. "And while I'm at it, I have to say you saved our asses, Tamika. And I, for one, am forever grateful."

A general murmur of appreciation went up. Adi raised their milkshake. "To Tamika for saving our asses, to Zeynep for the plan, and to Gabriel for being safe."

They clinked their beverages. Gabriel sucked on his milkshake and continued. "So, I followed her."

"Wait," said Zeynep. "How did you follow her if you didn't have a car?"

Gabriel stared at his milkshake. "The doors to Sally's Range Rover were all open. She was rearranging things. The car was on the street so there was a lot of noise. I slipped in the trunk. It's not really a trunk —more of a hatchback."

Tamika closed her eyes and shook her head.

"Don't worry, Auntie Ta. I was careful. Anyway, after we arrived at the house, I slipped out of the car and into the house. I heard a man's voice downstairs, so I ran upstairs."

"What did you hope to accomplish?" asked Tala.

"I wanted to find out why she had broken in. Maybe listen in on a conversation. Poke around. You know. My gut told me something wasn't right about Sally, so I wanted to find out more when she confirmed it by breaking into Adi's apartment."

Adi crunched on an onion ring. "Did you find anything?"

Gabriel smiled.

Tamika sighed. "Sometimes he can be so extra."

"I had to go upstairs because I couldn't hear anything downstairs—it was too risky. Upstairs, I found Sally's home office."

"But how did you get locked in there?" asked Katrina.

"When Sally went in the house, I went upstairs and naturally chose the office to search. I hid behind the door when Sally came in. She spent a few minutes on the computer and then she left, but not before she locked the door."

"Why would she lock the door?"

"I dunno. Maybe she kept valuable things in there? Who knows. Whatever the reason, I was trapped. I did make good use of the time, though, with the computer, since she'd left it on."

"So, what did you find?" Tala bit her lip.

"I searched for Aragon Partners to see if anything came up. All I got was my own story about them, and the follow-up articles. But one of the search results took me to the website of another construction company, Bickford, where the story was reposted. Sally had it bookmarked."

Tamika let out a low whistle. "Bickford—that name rings a bell. Didn't I see it on the major donors' list last year?"

Zeynep nodded and rubbed her forefinger and thumb.

"Wait a minute," said Katrina. "You already knew that, didn't you, Zeynep?"

She gave a little nod.

Gabriel's eyes grew wide. "But how did you know?"

"I'm an administrative assistant, remember? I have access to a lot of systems on campus. And I can assure you none of them are secure—fortunately for me."

"But what does it mean?" asked Adi.

"It means Bickford is our mark. And he's our mark for a reason."

"And that is?" asked Tala, looking lost.

"Of course!" Tamika snapped her fingers. "So that was what Dean Bullard was talking about at the party, with his wealthy local businesspeople. Bickford Developers is where the money comes from. Hit them, and you hit the trustees where it hurts."

"And Bickford were also in the running for the dorm room contract," said Zeynep.

"So what do we do now?" asked Adi.

"We're going to meet Mr. Bickford, pirate queens," said Tamika. "I received a text from Dean Bullard that he's set up a brunch meeting tomorrow. I've never seen the man move so fast."

Gabriel looked bewildered. "Pirate queens?"

22

———

"Are you alright?" Katrina put a hand on Zeynep's shoulder. Her friend's face was tight and pale, even in the warm glow of the sunshine and rich blue hue of the Zephyr restaurant sign.

"It's nothing. Just some complications with Batu." She scrolled through her texts.

"Do you want to go through with this?" asked Tala.

Zeynep nodded. "It won't help not to go through with it. Let's get a table."

Katrina walked up to the host. "We have a reservation for two tables. Would it be possible to have two of the high-back booths next to each other?"

"My name's Sarah." She snapped her gum.

"Yes, nice to meet you, Sarah," said Katrina. "May we have those booths next to each other?"

Sarah's eyes narrowed. "What for?"

"Oh, so we're near each other. But we have too many to fit into one."

Adi clicked their tongue. "Just give us the booths, will you?"

Katrina did a double take. As Sarah led them to the booths, Katrina said, "What's gotten into you, Adi? So direct."

Adi smiled. "Taking a page out of your book."

Tala and Tamika slid into the first booth, and Zeynep, Adi, and Katrina into the next. Gabriel had wanted to come along, but Tamika preferred he stayed at home because she was worried about him. She didn't know why, but she told him she had to trust her gut. They promised him they'd bring him home Zephyr's signature football-sized cinnamon bun, smothered in pecans and frosting. Katrina salivated at the thought. Must focus. But she was soon carried away by the fantasy of ordering everything on the plastic-covered menu in front of her.

Zeynep sipped her coffee and surveyed Katrina. "What are you going to order?"

"Why are you so interested?"

"Touchy this morning, aren't we?" said Adi, not looking up from the menu.

"I can't decide between the cinnamon bun and the leek and cheese omelets with potatoes."

"Let's order the cinnamon bun for the table and then you can also have the omelets."

Katrina brightened. "Excellent idea. I knew there was a reason you were head of the pirate queens."

Sarah snapped her gum. "What will you have?"

Katrina ordered the omelet and Zeynep ordered fruit and granola while Adi went for the French toast.

"Have the other guests arrived at the table next to us?" asked Katrina.

"What guests?" She chewed her gum as if it were a tiring chore.

"Never mind," said Zeynep, waving Sarah away.

Voices floated over the top of the booth.

"Dean Bullard, thanks for coming," Tamika was saying. Katrina realized they wouldn't be using first names in the presence of a student like Tala.

"My pleasure," said Dean Bullard. "Let me introduce Sidney Bickford, one of Blipton's major donors. Mr. Bickford, this is Tala and Professor Scott."

"Please call me Sidney."

Katrina froze. She leaned over, nearly dunking her hair in her coffee. "That's Ney—the man who was with Sally last night."

Zeynep nodded. Katrina's mouth hung open. Did the woman know everything?

"After we order, we'll get down to business," said Dean Bullard.

Distracted by the arrival of their own food, Katrina tuned out the other table's orders. She bit into the soft, gooey cheese and leek omelet. Delicious.

"So," said Dean Bullard. "I told Sidney about your proposition here, and he's very interested."

"Oh, absolutely. Anything for a good cause, isn't that right, Doug?" Sidney broke in with a chuckle. "But if you don't mind—er—Professor, I'd like to know about your guarantees."

"What guarantees?" asked Tamika.

"What happens if people find out about the algorithm?"

"Why would they?"

Zeynep, Adi, and Katrina smiled at one another.

"No reason. I just want to know. I trust my intuition."

"You're right to do that. I—" Tamika broke off, as if she were stopping herself. "Due to the nature of the project, though, we can't give you any ironclad guarantees. All we're doing is offering the algorithm. We can promise the two of us will be quiet."

Ping. Katrina looked at her phone. A message from Zeynep? But why would she send a text when she was sitting right there?

She tapped the message. It was just one word: *Sneeze.*

Katrina shot Zeynep a questioning glance. Zeynep nodded back.

Taking a deep breath, Katrina held a hand to her nose and let out a delicate "achoo!" But Zeynep's frown told her it hadn't been up to the mark. She tried again, this time with a more robust sneeze.

Adi's fork clattered on the plate.

Silence reigned at the booth next to them.

"Is that enough for you?" said Tamika in a loud voice.

"Wait a minute," said Dean Bullard.

They heard a slithering noise. Then a shadow fell across the table.

Adi's face was scrunched up like a gargoyle. Zeynep's eyes were closed. Katrina turned her face to the wall.

"It's you. What are you all doing here?"

"Oh, Dean Bullard. How nice to see you," said Zeynep. "We're having brunch. I said to Katrina it sounded like you. What a coincidence!"

The dean grinned at them with his inane smile. "It is indeed a coincidence."

A leprechaun head popped over the top of the booth. It was very clearly the man they had seen last night at Sally's house. His eyes narrowed as he surveyed Katrina. "Why, hello. Haven't I met you before? I don't recognize your face, and yet..."

"You must have noticed me on campus. I'm a history professor. And this is Zeynep Zaman, administrative assistant, and Adi Tobias, in student development."

Sidney pursed his lips.

"Well, shall we get back to our brunch? Nice to see you all," said Dean Bullard, as if he did believe this was all a coincidence. He would. The man's cauliflower ears certainly indicated a cauliflower brain.

As they all went back to the booth, Adi covered their face.

"So are you in or are you out, Mr. Bickford?" asked Tamika.

"I'll have to think about it, Professor Scott. Something isn't right."

23

———

Adi revved the engine on the Corolla. A satisfying roar died as quickly as it had begun.

"Quick! Bickford's getting into his car." Tala hopped in the back seat.

Adi turned the key again. Nothing.

Tamika groaned through gritted teeth. "We'll have to squeeze into my Mini."

"No way," said Katrina, who felt like a small child as soon as she said it. "Adi—try the engine again."

"We have no choice," said Zeynep. "Besides, Katrina, you get shotgun since you're the tallest."

Fortunately, Tamika's red Mini was parked alongside the Corolla. After a few false starts, Zeynep, Tala, and Adi squeezed into the back.

"Clown car ready for liftoff," said Katrina.

"Don't you dare call my Mini a clown car. I had to work hard for this."

———

BICKFORD'S blue BMW glided out of the parking lot, away from downtown and the university.

"Remind me why we're following him? Are we going to force him to buy the algorithm?" asked Katrina.

"Funny, Katrina. Since he's nervous about the deal, I want to see what he does," said Zeynep.

"What will it tell us?" asked Adi.

They turned off the main road.

"Well, so far we know he's not going home. He lives in the opposite direction," said Zeynep.

"Why are we climbing Snake's Canyon?" asked Tala. "Does anyone live up here?"

"Uber-rich people live up here," said Adi. "Does Bickford have another house, Zeynep?"

Zeynep scrolled through her phone. "I'm looking through all the addresses I have." She stopped. "I'm getting carsick."

"I'll take a look," said Adi. Zeynep handed her the phone.

Katrina winced as they took a sharp curve. She peered out the window into the void and quickly moved her head back to focus on the road ahead of them.

Katrina glanced in the rearview mirror. Tala had her head between her knees.

"Tamika, ah, you'd better pull over," mumbled Zeynep.

"Why?"

"Tala and Zeynep need to get out. Now," said Adi. "Unless you want your Mini to be ruined."

"But we'll lose the BMW." Tamika gripped the wheel like a race car driver. Katrina smiled at her singular focus. "There's a vista point in a few yards. We can pull off there."

They came to a halt in a cloud of dust. Zeynep and Tala tumbled out of the car. Adi closed their door. "That's better. I get violently ill when someone else vomits."

Katrina turned around. "You are sensitive, aren't you?"

"And proud of it," smiled Adi.

Tamika hit the steering wheel. "Damn. We'll never find him now."

Tala and Zeynep slid into the back seat. "Better now," said Tala. "We can keep going."

Tamika twisted the steering wheel hard and skidded out of the parking lot and back onto the winding road.

"We've lost him," sighed Tamika.

"Keep driving," said Zeynep.

After a few more hairpin turns, they spotted the blue BMW, parked in the driveway of a Tudor-style house overlooking the town below.

"What's the address?" asked Adi.

"Slow down, speed racer," said Katrina.

Tamika shifted the gears and slowed to a crawl. "I have to keep moving. There's a car behind me."

Katrina barely made out the numbers on the house. "1343. I suppose this is Snake's Canyon Road."

Tamika pulled over as best she could and rolled down their windows—just a crack. Bickford whistled as he approached the door to the house.

"Aha!" said Adi after a few moments of tapping the phone. Then they let out a low whistle. "Google is genius. And Zeynep has a magic address list. You'll never guess who lives here."

"I hate guessing games, Adi," said Katrina.

Zeynep and Tala, though recovered, were silent.

"Joe Aragon. Of Aragon Partners," said Adi.

Tamika drove up the road, made a three-point turn in a tight driveway and cruised back to Aragon's house, making use of the shoulder on the right-hand side.

"Why are we waiting?" asked Katrina.

"See? That's why we're waiting." Zeynep pointed at Sidney Bickford, who stalked out of the house. He got into his car, slammed the door and then smacked the steering wheel. Then he screeched out of the driveway, gravel hissing from his tires in a furious spray.

———

GABRIEL THREW one arm off the side of the couch and scrolled with the other. No messages. He put down the phone and closed his eyes. Frustrated by being left out of the loop, he consoled himself by visualizing Zephyr's cinnamon roll they had promised him.

A knock came at the door.

Gabriel jerked up and stared at it.

The knock came again, not loud, but certainly firm.

Grateful for the carpet, Gabriel ice-skated silently across to the door and spied through the peephole.

He shrank back.

He'd recognize that mane anywhere. Dean Hackett.

"Good morning, Adi," Hackett said through the door.

Mind racing, Gabriel considered his options. His need for security lost out to his journalist's curiosity.

He flung open the door.

In that moment, Gabriel decided it was all worth it to see Hackett's mouth hang open.

"Ah, Gabriel Lomax, isn't it?" Hackett unbuttoned his blazer. "Is Adi in?" Then his eyes narrowed. "And what are you doing here? I thought you were in the hospital."

Gabriel turned on his innocent cherubic charm. "I've recovered, Dean Hackett. And Adi asked me to watch their cat—they had to be somewhere all day, and possibly overnight. Can I give Adi a message?"

Hackett looked over his shoulder. "I see. May I come in?"

Gabriel hesitated. "Why? If you wanted to visit Adi, they're not here. Why come in?"

"I've been meaning to talk to you about something, young man. Might as well do it now."

Hackett's tall frame filled the door. It was clear he wasn't going anywhere.

"Okay, but let me call Adi. They'll want to know you were here."

"I'd rather Adi not know the two of us were chatting."

Hackett slipped into the apartment, shut the door and leaned against it.

Furbaby ambled into the room. She blinked, halted, and hissed at Hackett.

"Adi's cat doesn't like me."

Gabriel's stomach twisted and tightened. "Furbaby can detect people's energy. It seems your energy is not exactly positive."

"Baloney," said Hackett, making himself at home on the couch. At least the dean wasn't spitting out swear words. Yet.

Gabriel patted Furbaby and then stood near the couch.

"Sit down. No need to hover over me."

Gabriel sat down and turned on his phone. Hackett snatched it. He pulled his lips back, revealing unnaturally pale gums and very white teeth. His face had become a blotchy mess of pink, white, and red.

"Hey! What are you doing?"

"I don't want you distracted from what I have to say. I give my life to Blipton University, trying to keep it afloat. You have no idea how hard my job is."

Despite the inner tumult in his digestive system, Gabriel sat quietly and stared at Hackett.

Hackett rose and paced behind the couch. "Every day, there are complaints from the staff, faculty, and students. And I have to deal with all of them! If that isn't enough, meddlers like you and professors who shall remain nameless create all these unnecessary problems for me. Like dealing with the publicity around the developers and the dorms." Hackett threw his hands up. "I mean, who gives a fuck? You all want the dorms built, don't you? Who cares if it's a bunch of lazy good-for-nothings who get thrown out. Good riddance to bad rubbish is what I say."

Gabriel blinked. Keep him talking, he thought. Let him rant.

The front doorknob rattled.

Furbaby hissed again.

When Gabriel turned his head from the door back to Hackett, he gasped.

A silver gun was aimed directly at his chest.

24

Gabriel backed away. He called, "I'm coming. Let me get the door!"

Clutching the gun, Hackett waved it at Gabriel, motioning him to the door. Hackett slipped into one of the back rooms.

With trembling fingers, Gabriel unlocked the door.

Adi smiled and held up a large paper bag. "Your cinnamon roll has arrived, sir."

Tamika pushed past Adi. "What's wrong, baby? You're shaking." She grabbed both of his arms.

Gabriel opened his mouth, but nothing came out.

Tamika pulled Gabriel and Adi from the door, back into the hallway. She shut the door and stroked Gabriel's shoulder. "Calm down, sweetie, and tell Auntie Ta what happened."

Gabriel sucked in a great breath of air and blew it out. "H-H-H-Hackett is here. In the back. With a gun."

"What?!" yelled Katrina.

"Shhhh!" said Zeynep.

"I'll kill him," whispered Katrina.

Adi adjusted their glasses. "There are only two bedrooms, plus the bathroom. He should have discovered the fire escape by now, so let's go in. I don't want to leave my Furbaby alone with him."

"Good point," said Katrina, thinking she would personally murder the entire university if anyone laid a hand on her Pumpkin.

They inched into the apartment and split up when they reached the hallway.

Katrina peered out the open window at the fire escape. The curtains blew in the breeze.

Hackett had vanished.

———

GABRIEL MUNCHED on the cinnamon roll. "If you all hadn't come, I don't know what would have happened."

"So let me get this straight," said Katrina, eyeing the cinnamon roll. "Hackett comes here, presumably to threaten Adi—"

"Or to get information from Adi," said Zeynep.

"And then decides to threaten you. Then he pulls the gun. The man must be completely delusional."

"Remember, he did try to talk or do something to Gabriel in the hospital," said Tamika.

"It's strange." Gabriel wiped his hands on a napkin. "It's like he wanted me to listen and to stop asking questions. That's all. Though he was terrifying, I didn't get the impression he actually wanted to hurt me."

"Yeah, whatever. The man is a nut," said Katrina.

"Gabriel's onto something," said Zeynep. "Hackett's unbalanced for sure. He thinks he's doing everything to save the university. Which means we need to convince him we're trying to do the same."

Just then Zeynep's phone chimed. She glanced at it and let out a quick, satisfied snort.

"Good news?" Adi asked.

"Yep," said Zeynep, her fingers already busy tapping out a reply.

"So how do we convince Hackett we're on his side?" asked Tala.

"What if we get him in on the algorithm deal? It might distract him from his other antics."

"Such as trying to kill me?" asked Katrina. "Remember, the man cut my car brakes."

"We don't know that for sure," said Adi.

"Who else would do it?" Katrina's face grew warm.

"It doesn't really matter," said Zeynep. She looked at Katrina and said hurriedly, "I don't mean it doesn't matter, I mean it doesn't matter for what we're trying to accomplish. If we can get him in on this deal, he'll be distracted by trying to make it work."

"Won't it make everything more complicated?" asked Tamika.

Heads nodded.

"It will, but the man has a gun, and I'm afraid he'll come back later to try to *persuade* Adi."

Adi gulped their water and banged down the glass as if they had just finished their fourth shot of vodka.

"I'm sold. Let's get Hackett in on the deal. Maybe he can convince Bickford, too."

"But how do we get him in on it?" Tala's legs jiggled.

"Are you alright, Tala?" asked Katrina.

"Fine."

She was anything but fine. But it was clear Tala wasn't going to talk until she was ready.

"Though Bickford has cold feet, Bullard is still thrilled about the plan. If we can get Bullard to rope in Hackett, it should do the trick," said Zeynep.

"But what about Bickford talking to Aragon? What does it mean?"

"I have no idea, but I can't imagine it has anything to do with the algorithm. It must have to do with the scandal over the developers and the dorms," said Zeynep.

Tamika's phone buzzed. "We might have the answer," she said. "It's Bickford."

She held the phone up to her ear. "Hello, yes, this is Professor Scott." She paused. "Oh no, Sidney, don't worry about it. We understand." Katrina heard rapid-fire chattering. "We? I mean the royal 'we.' Tala and I. Do you mind if I put you on speakerphone so Tala can hear as well?"

Tamika slid the phone onto the coffee table.

"Hello, Tala. I was telling Professor Scott I wanted to apologize for ending our meeting so abruptly. I had to think."

"Not a problem, Mr. Bickford. We understand it's a lot to think about," said Tala.

Adi sneezed.

"Bless you," said Sidney.

"Thank you," said Tamika and Tala together. They both winced.

"Anyway, I've been thinking," said Sidney. "I like the sound of your deal. But I'm hesitating about it because I'm the only one in on it. I'd feel better if someone else were going to pay, too. You know, sort of insurance. Especially because if this ever became public, I'd be finished."

Zeynep scribbled on a scrap of paper. She slid it to Tamika. Tamika nodded.

"What if Dean Bullard, or maybe even another dean, got in on the deal? It would be a kind of collateral. If it did all collapse, they'd not only lose their reputations, they'd lose their jobs."

Sidney smacked his lips. Silence.

Furbaby meowed. Adi scooped her up and took her into the kitchen.

"Bullard owes me a few favors. And I know he has stacks of cash since he's a tight-fisted—" He stopped himself. "And what is this you said about another dean? Do you know another dean who'd be interested?"

"Oh, I just put that out there. Let me think," said Tamika, smiling at the crew. "There's Dean Aponte and Dean Napier."

"They're too straitlaced. Besides, I don't think either of them has any money," said Sidney.

"How about Dean Hackett?"

"Now you're talking. Hackett is fanatical in his devotion to the university."

"That he is," said Tamika.

25

———————

Pumpkin's wet nose rubbed Katrina's face. Katrina wiped it with her blanket. "I know, Kins, I missed you, too. Sorry I had to leave you for so long, but I'm sure you wreaked havoc in the backyard, didn't you?"

Pumpkin flicked his tail and trotted off.

"No need to get huffy. I'll get up and feed you, Your Highness."

Katrina sat up and rubbed her stiff neck. She'd fallen asleep on the couch the night before because she knew she could make a quick exit out the back door in case anyone tried to break in. There was no escape from her bedroom. Though she doubted she would have slept well, even if she'd been in her own bed. Her head was in a heavy brain fog.

Pumpkin meowed. Then he started his low guttural meow, a sure sign he felt persecuted.

"Alright! Alright! I hear you, beastie." She lumbered into the kitchen, turned on the coffee, and popped a Zephyr cinnamon roll in the microwave. On her way home from Adi's yesterday, she'd decided she'd need one for the next morning. Must keep her strength up, not to mention her blood sugar.

Soon the kitchen was filled with the warm smell of coffee and cinnamon, along with the reassuring sounds of the gurgling coffeepot and the cat licking his wet food with complete abandon. She almost convinced herself the past few days hadn't happened. She battled with the urge to check her phone but decided that whatever had happened during the night would wait. Someone would have knocked on her door had it been really urgent.

After the first bite of cinnamon roll and sip of coffee, she caved in and picked up her phone. The screen lit up with a series of texts. She groaned. "Kins, they're bothering me again," she whined. Pumpkin's face remained inside his food bowl.

"You're so mean," she sighed, scrolling through the texts. She should be grateful all of this had happened during the night, without her having to be involved.

Are you up?

No

Yes

Yes

Bickford said he contacted Hackett. It's a go

Great!

What happens next?

Bickford says he wants us to meet at his place at 11 am

Just us?

He didn't say

How are we going to give him the algorithm?

Tala's got it all on a USB stick. But she'll need access to Blipton's Admissions computer system to install it

How can a donor get access?

A donor can't, but a dean can.

How will we get there?

We have to go in Tamika's Mini. The Corolla's busted and so is Katrina's car.

I'll pick you all up. Tala, Adi, Zeynep, and then Katrina.

KATRINA GLANCED AT THE CLOCK. Ten a.m. She showered, dressed in all black, and had just enough time to finish the cinnamon roll with reheated coffee before she heard the Mini's horn beeping.

"Be good, Kins. I hope to be back soon. If not, I bequeath everything I own to you."

Pumpkin licked his paw, looked up, and then went back to grooming.

Katrina slammed the front door.

Zeynep got out of the front seat, gave Katrina a hug, and squeezed into the back.

"Good morning!" chirped Tamika. "And how did you sleep last night?"

"Why are you so damn cheerful this morning? I can't have been the only one not to get a wink last night."

General murmurs of agreement came from the back seat.

"See?" Katrina waved her hand. "They're all grumpy. What's with you?"

"I had a vision."

Katrina groaned.

"Ignore her, Tamika," croaked Adi from the back seat. "Tell us about your vision."

Tamika licked her lips and shifted the gears. "Well, it came to me as I was drifting off."

"That's lucid dreaming. There's a scientific explanation," said Katrina.

"Hush, Katrina!" Zeynep yelled from the back seat.

"Anyway," said Tamika. "I had this vision of all of us sitting together on a train."

"You mean Amtrak?" asked Katrina.

"I think so. It looked like an Amtrak setup. We were all sitting in the lounge, toasting our success."

"I've never been on a train!" cried Tala, suddenly coming alive. "Are we going on a train?"

"It's symbolic," said Katrina. "Who's a dream interpretation expert?"

"Hold on," said Adi. "I'll google it. It says a train dream means you're going in the right direction or that you're worrying about a situation which will turn out fine. In other words, it means to stop worrying."

"I'll take it," said Katrina. "Either way, it's a good omen, isn't it?"

"It had better be," said Zeynep as they arrived at Bickford's sprawling mansion on the outskirts of town. A golden retriever came up to greet them. Tala crouched down and hugged the dog. Adi did as well.

"I thought you were a cat person, Adi," said Katrina.

"I like both. I don't discriminate, unlike some people," said Adi.

"Touché," replied Katrina.

"Can we focus?" Zeynep's hands flew up.

Everyone murmured "sorry" and stood at attention.

Zeynep paced back and forth. "I don't think he can hear us. The driveway is too long." She took a deep breath. "Here's the plan. Tala has the algorithm. She'll incorporate it into Bickford's system once he gives us the money and the login information."

"But we can't all go in," said Adi. "He'll be suspicious."

"Yes, you'll all wait in the car with the engine running."

"What if something goes wrong? Should we go in?"

"How about this? If we're not out by eleven thirty, and you haven't received a text from me, then you all should come in."

"But what will we do if we come in? We don't have any weapons," said Katrina.

"I put a crowbar in the trunk, just in case," said Zeynep.

They all looked in awe at Zeynep. She gave them a slight smile.

"Alright. Let's do it!" Tala clapped her hands and slid on her backpack.

26

Tala hung back as Tamika pushed the doorbell, relieved that the professor was taking the lead. Another dog barked inside. The golden retriever barked in return. Tala rolled her head around her shoulders.

Tamika put a hand on her shoulder. "You'll be fine. Just remember you know more than anyone in the room about computers." She chuckled. "A lot more."

"But what if this is all a setup?"

"Look. I could sense that if it were true." She paused. "It's a simple operation—pretend you're helping someone fix their computer."

Tala nodded, though her last meal rumbled rebelliously in her stomach.

Sidney Bickford flung open the door, holding back a small poodle. "Don't mind Mandy. She gets a little excited with new visitors." Bickford was dressed in a long flowered guayabera shirt.

"You look summery," said Tamika approvingly.

"Oh, yes, this is just to celebrate. Thought the occasion called for it." He let go of the poodle and she sprang into the hallway. "Come in, come in." He shut the door and pointed to the corridor. Tamika's heels clicked across the tiled floor. In the living room doorway, she stopped so suddenly Tala bumped into her.

Tala fought the urge to turn and run.

There, on the couch, sat Deans Hackett and Bullard. Hackett was smoking and sipping coffee. Bullard stuffed his face with pineapple and cantaloupe.

"Please, make yourself at home. I have fruit and coffee. If you'd like anything else, I can arrange that too." Bickford was seemingly oblivious to the awkwardness of the situation.

As Tala and Tamika lowered themselves slowly onto the slippery black leather sofa, Bickford said, "Your faces tell me you weren't expecting the deans to be here. But I thought it only appropriate since they're putting up their hard-earned cash, too."

Bullard nodded and mumbled through a mouthful of strawberry. Hackett lifted his chin in recognition of their presence and stubbed out his cigarette.

A tiny Chihuahua scuttled into the room and sat down in front of Tala, staring at her. Though her first impulse was to coo over the tiny creature, she just stared back.

Breathe, Tala, breathe. Everyone and everything in here is trying to unnerve you.

Hackett slammed down his mug so hard Tala was sure it would smash the glass coffee table to pieces.

Bickford looked at him and slapped his knees. "Now. Shall we get down to business? I believe you have the algorithm." He peered expectantly at Tala.

"I'll need access to the main server. I assume one of you brought a laptop?" Tala looked from Hackett to Bullard.

Hackett reached one hand behind the sofa and returned with an open laptop. "I'm already logged in," he said, sliding it across the coffee table.

Tala plugged her in her USB stick and clicked furiously at the keyboard.

Tamika put her hand on Tala's arm. "Wait. We need the money first."

Bickford nodded at the deans.

They looked at each other for a moment and nodded.

"Do you mind? We need to speak to each other for a moment." Without waiting for a reply, Hackett stalked into the bedroom and Bullard trundled after.

Tala surveyed Bickford's face—he looked pretty good for an old person, though not as good as Tamika. His forehead was smooth, save two number eleven frown lines that could make him appear more serious than his jovial nature indicated.

Tamika rose, crossed her arms and walked to an enormous window, the clacking of her heels sounding remarkably similar to the Chihuahua, who still stared patiently at Tala.

She cleared her throat. "What's your dog's name?"

The frown lines disappeared, though Tala wasn't sure if it was because of the dog or because Hackett and Bullard had returned.

"The Chihuahua's name is Laura Ann, the retriever is Georgina, and the poodle is Mandy. Though I usually just call them by various ridiculous nicknames."

"Georgina is a beautiful name," said Tala.

"Aren't you going to ask how I named them?"

Tamika spun around. "Actually, I was. Tell us and then let's get this business over with."

Bickford pulled back his lips slightly, causing Tala to lean back, though her back remained ramrod straight.

"They're all victims of serial killers. I thought it'd be a nice way to keep their memories alive."

"You're one sick bastard, Bickford," snorted Hackett with a mixture of admiration and disgust.

Bullard remained silent, though his eyes bulged.

Tamika smiled and pointed a finger at Bickford. "You're joking, aren't you? You wouldn't really do that."

Bickford leaned back his head and laughed. Wiping his eyes, he said, "There's a reason you're a professor, Dr. Scott. Georgina is her real name, but not the rest. My little joke, as you say."

Tala blinked and stared in wonder. Was this some sort of test? Were these people their impending robot overlords?

She was brought back to reality by the click of a briefcase. Bullard spun around to face Tala and Tamika. Tala's eyes widened at the thick stacks of notes.

With forced coolness, Tamika took up individual stacks of greenbacks and flipped through them. Tala did the same with the other briefcase. The largest stack of notes she'd ever seen in her life was the wad of five-dollar bills her mom had given her before she left for college. Now, here she was, flipping through this lovely money. And yet...she wondered how her dad would react. He'd probably think she was a thief.

Tamika patted her hand and smiled. Tala pushed away her unprofitable—literally unprofitable—thoughts and focused on the task at hand.

"Where's your money, Bickford?" asked Hackett.

"Mine is not so neatly arranged as yours. I wanted to leave it in the safe until we all arrived." He got up and retreated to the hallway.

"I need multiple logins, Dean Hackett. Do you have them saved somewhere on the desktop?"

Tamika hoped Hackett was lazy enough that he had made a list of his passwords on the computer. Even though it seemed to be every day they all received university email warnings about yet another administrator or professor who had their laptop stolen with all their passwords easily accessible from the same computer.

"No, no," said Hackett. "Surely you don't think I'd be so careless as all that." His toe tapped out an irregular beat on the carpet.

Tamika chuckled. "If there's one thing I know about faculty and administrators, we're too busy to keep track of our passwords—or we think we are. I'm calling your bluff, Hackett."

Tala browsed around the laptop. Bam. There it was: a file named pwds2018.docx. How cryptic. She copied it over to the thumb drive while Hackett was still raking his memory for the login details.

"I just remembered. I think I saved a few yesterday on a document —temporarily, of course."

"Of course, Dean Hackett." Tala smiled. "I already found it."

Hackett hissed, "You two bitches better be on the level."

Dean Bullard choked on his apple slice. He looked at Hackett as if seeing him for the first time. "No need for that tone, Hackett."

Tala's jaw relaxed for the first time since they'd walked in the door. Hackett was on the defensive, because she was sure those passwords applied to more than just the university system.

"What, are you trying to be all self-righteous now?" asked Hackett.

Tala and Tamika glanced at each other.

"No. I know we're both doing this for the good of the university," said Bullard. "I don't think there's a need for such language."

Tamika stood up. "We can take care of ourselves, thank you very much. We don't need your insults or patronizing behavior." She snapped the cases shut and grabbed one. Catching her eye, Tala slid the USB stick out of the laptop and into her pocket, while she took the other briefcase. Time for them to make their getaway.

Hackett grabbed Tamika's hand. "You'd better put down the briefcase. Leave it on the table until Bickford comes back."

Tamika stared at his hand. He let go and then she let go of the case and sat back down.

Tala fought the urge to swing her case at Hackett's head, reminding herself she would have had the same reaction had she been in his position. Not that she'd ever be in his position. Not for a million dollars.

Bullard speared a blackberry. "Bickford's taking a long time." He swallowed. "Where is he?"

"Here I am." Bickford stood in the hallway, smiling and looking jovial in his colorful shirt.

With a gun.

Katrina looked at her phone. "Where are they? It's eleven forty-five. Should we go in?"

"Let's wait," said Zeynep.

"But Tamika said we should go in if she didn't send us a text by eleven forty-five," said Adi.

"I say we wait. These things take a while, and I wouldn't be surprised if Tala and Tamika were distracted by the money."

Katrina played with the door handle. "I dunno..." she grumbled. "Something is wrong." She opened the door and got out.

"Where are you going?" asked Zeynep.

"To get the crowbar," said Katrina. "I'm going in."

"Don't be ridiculous, Katrina," said Adi. "Besides, we all agreed Zeynep calls the shots."

"I agree in principle, but Tamika and Tala are in danger." She popped the trunk and grabbed the nasty-looking crowbar. She'd only seen them in movies but was sure she'd only need to threaten Bickford with it.

"Katrina, put the crowbar back in the trunk," said Zeynep in a low warning voice.

Katrina stood still, her hand wrapped around the crowbar. She had no idea what her next step should be. She took a step toward the driveway. Before she knew what was happening, Zeynep had grabbed the crowbar and Adi had pulled her hands behind her back.

"What the hell are you doing?" hissed Katrina.

"Saving you from messing this up," said Zeynep.

Katrina heard the crowbar clatter to the ground behind her. Her head jerked up. Sidney Bickford was opening his front door.

"Quick!" said Adi. "Get in the car!" They scrambled into the car and crouched down. Katrina peeped up over the edge of the window. "He's got a gun!" she hissed. She watched him stuff the gun in a jacket pocket as he opened the trunk of his blue BMW. He threw in two briefcases, slammed it and got into the car.

"What do we do?" asked Adi.

"We wait until he drives off," said Zeynep.

"Won't he spot us?" asked Katrina.

"He's too distracted to notice," said Zeynep. "Even if he does look in our direction, all he'll notice is an empty car. It's what he expects to see."

She heard the car backing up the driveway. Fast. Then it screeched and sped past them, down the hill.

Adi began to whimper. "They're probably dead."

"Pull yourself together. They'll be fine. Follow me. Katrina, make sure you grab the crowbar."

They ran down the driveway, just in time to hear a shot ring out.

27

———

Ten minutes earlier

"YOU STUPID, STUPID, STUPID BITCHES," cursed Hackett.

"Hey!" Bickford moved closer, with the gun still pointed at Hackett. "I do not abide by sexist language. And don't even think about your racist epithets."

Tamika found herself surveying the network of broken capillaries on Hackett's nose. Odd the little things one noticed when death was upon one. A sense of calm washed over her. Though her hands were in the air so she couldn't give Tala a reassuring pat, she gave her a smile. Tala's strained face tried, unsuccessfully, to smile back.

"Now, Professor Scott, I need you to take the rope in the rolltop desk right here to my left. There's also scissors and duct tape. I need you to tie up the deans, then tie up Tala. Make sure you put your handbag near me."

He trained the gun on her as she did so.

"Why do you trust her? Is she in on this?" asked Bullard.

"No, you ninny. Look at her dress."

Tamika peered down at herself, as if she couldn't recall what she was wearing.

"Her dress is so fitted there's not a chance she'd hide a gun or some other weapon in it. That's why I'm telling her to put her handbag next to me."

Tamika went over to the desk, still in the line of sight of Bickford. She removed the rope, tape, and scissors. Even though she was terrified, she found great pleasure in making the rope so tight around Hackett's wrists that he let out a little yelp.

Bickford smiled. "You deserve it for your bad behavior, Hackett."

"What about me?" whined Bullard. "I haven't done anything wrong."

"You're criminally incompetent."

"What's the matter with you, Bickford? I thought you wanted that contract for the new dorms?" asked Bullard.

"I did—until I found out what else I'd have to do to get it. That contract would have ruined me and my company, Bullard, and you know it."

Tamika saw Tala finally smile, even as she had to put rope around her wrists.

"Make sure you don't go too easy on her, Tamika." Bickford inspected her handiwork and nodded approval. "Now it's your turn."

She sat on the couch as Bickford quickly tied the rope around her wrists. She debated telling him there were people in the driveway, waiting to save her. No, it would be suicidal to tell him.

As soon as Bickford finished tying up Tamika, he grabbed the briefcases and gun, stopping only to click a few buttons on the stereo system. "I'm afraid I'll have to leave you all now. I wouldn't alert the police as you'll have to explain what you're doing here. Besides, I set up some safeguards to alert the police about you paying me off for an algorithm."

"But are you going to leave us?" asked Bullard.

"I'm afraid so. I've arranged for an associate to come by in a few hours to let you all go. After I've had enough time to make my escape."

———

THE DOOR WAS UNLOCKED. Katrina pushed it, letting it open on its own.

She heard voices. Tamika and Tala's voice. And Hackett and Bullard's.

They tiptoed in. Katrina screamed as she saw Tamika and Tala tied up. She ran to them, grabbed the scissors on the side table, and quickly untied them.

Hackett and Bullard stared at Katrina.

"Aren't you going to untie us as well?" Hackett spat out the words.

"I'm not sure," said Tamika. "You probably have a gun. And then where'd we be at?"

Hackett mumbled under his breath.

"What's that? I can't hear you!" said Katrina. Despite the general horror of the situation, she was enjoying herself.

"Did you plan this?" asked Bullard. His eyes turned glassy.

"No, we didn't plan this," said Katrina. "We're as surprised as you are. Looks like we're out of a deal, but you two are out of much more."

"We'll get our money back," said Bullard confidentially.

"How?" asked Zeynep.

"We'll have the police find him."

"And how will you explain to the police what happened here? Besides, you voluntarily gave him the money, remember?"

"Well, at least you finished inputting the algorithm, right, Tala? We paid for it," said Hackett.

"You may have paid for it, but you paid Bickford, not us. We'll take our algorithm elsewhere, thank you very much," said Tala.

Hackett spluttered, unable to speak.

"At least let us go," whined Bullard. "I don't have a gun. I've never even seen one until today."

"Sorry," said Zeynep. "If we let you go, you'd probably untie Hackett. And the last thing we need is a maniac waving a gun at us."

"Don't worry," said Tamika. "Someone will be by to let you go.

Remember what Bickford said? Now, if you'll excuse us, I'd rather not run into one of Bickford's associates."

"What if no one comes?" asked Bullard. "I have an important meeting this afternoon."

"Wait a minute," said Katrina. "What was the gunshot we heard?"

"Bickford turned on his stereo before he left. He must have prerecorded a gunshot," said Tamika.

"But why?" asked Katrina.

"So the neighbors would call the police," said Zeynep.

They looked at one another.

"We'd better run for it," said Katrina.

"So long, suckers," said Tamika. "Have fun trying to explain this mess to the police."

28

"All aboard!"

Katrina scanned the station. No suspicious henchmen lurked in the shadows. They were really leaving on a train. And thanks to Zeynep, who had waved some sort of administrator's magic wand, they didn't have to travel coach. It wasn't exactly a luxurious liner, but Katrina did have an affection for Amtrak nonetheless.

Batu pecked her on each cheek. "We'll miss you. Come back soon."

Katrina's heart melted a little, and for the first time that week, she had an urge to stay.

Gabriel enfolded her in a tight hug. "Thank you for everything, Professor Frost. Please bring Auntie Ta back soon."

"You're surely not staying in the same dorm as before, are you?"

Gabriel's glowing face made it clear he was not. "Batu's new apartment has plenty of space, so he said I should move in with him. I miss having pets, so taking care of all of your cats will make me miss you all a little less."

"If you end up with a job in town, you're welcome to stay in my house. The people living there will move out in six months."

"Thanks. I'd like to get out of Snake's Canyon, but it might make sense to stay for a while."

Tamika gave him a light punch in the arm. "What do you mean, leave Snake's Canyon?"

"Aren't you leaving, Auntie Ta?"

"Watch your tongue, young man. I'm leaving on a self-imposed sabbatical. We'll be back soon."

Katrina smiled and nodded, though she wasn't sure they'd be back all that soon. Though she might have to slip back to make sure Pumpkin wasn't furious with her.

The train attendant ticked off their names. Katrina had thought it would be better to use fake names, but Zeynep rightly pointed out they hardly had time to doctor fake IDs. "I don't think anyone will come after us," she'd said, "but even if they did, they'd have a lookout at airports or on the highway. No one would ever dream of escaping on a train. Too slow and you never know if it will really ever show up!"

This train to New York was already forty-five minutes late. Katrina smiled at the pirate queens, all clad in sunglasses and summer clothing.

"Your compartments are on the upper level, right next to one another," said the dapper young attendant. "My name is Carlos, and I shall be at your service for the duration of the trip into New York. I'll arrive with mimosas after we get underway."

He helped them into the train car. They waved and blew kisses to Batu and Gabriel. Batu wiped away a tear.

As they wound up the small staircase, Tamika said, "Tala, dear, I believe you have an admirer."

Katrina chuckled. "Carlos stared at you during the introduction."

Tala said nothing.

"Don't tease her," said Adi.

Katrina lifted her suitcase onto the luggage rack inside their compartment. Not bad. Couch-like seats faced one another in a long, narrow compartment. A basket of fruit and cookies stood on the small pullout table.

"It's not that," said Tala. "I'm worried about my parents." She slumped down onto a seat.

"I planned to tell you when we got comfortable," said Zeynep. "I received a text from the lawyer we hired for your parents. He said he's hopeful the deportation proceedings will be dropped. When I asked him what 'hopeful' meant, he said he was a lawyer so he wouldn't promise anything, but that we could breathe easy for now."

Tala flung her arms around Zeynep. "Thank you, thank you! I feel better. I've been so nervous."

"But the situation hasn't changed in a while. I noticed earlier you were worried," said Katrina. "Why did you become so nervous all of a sudden?"

"I found a letter from my mom to my dad, from when they were first dating. Something about it made me feel so guilty. As if the deportation proceedings were my fault."

"But why would you think they're your fault?" asked Adi.

"Because when I applied for federal funding this year, almost as soon as I sent in the application, Immigration showed up and took my parents away. It was too much of a coincidence."

"It probably was a coincidence—not that I'd put anything past Immigration, you know," said Zeynep. "Even if it were true, it's still not your fault. Anything might have triggered an investigation."

"You're right. But now that we've hired a lawyer, I feel better." Tala's cheerful expression held a hint of puzzlement. "By the way, Zeynep, you never told me where that money for his fees came from."

"Or how we came to be traveling first class," Katrina added. Four pairs of eyes looked at Zeynep expectantly.

The loudspeaker beeped. "Welcome aboard. We'll be underway shortly. Please stay in your compartments until the conductor arrives to check your tickets. Thank you."

The conductor popped his head around the door. "Tickets, please."

Wordlessly, Zeynep handed over a stack of tickets.

The conductor frowned under a glossy, bushy mustache.

"Would Katrina Frost, Zeynep Zaman, and Tamika Scott please come with me? Thank you."

———

Katrina's left hand shook as she followed the conductor. A montage of police films and TV shows flashed across the screen of her mind. This was it. They were going to jail.

"What's the matter, conductor?" asked Zeynep in a curious and calm voice.

He pointed at an empty compartment. "Please, have a seat."

They filed in and sat down.

The conductor handed them their tickets.

He frowned.

Then he laughed. "You three look like you've seen a ghost!"

Katrina glanced at Zeynep and Tamika. They both blinked.

"You were in the wrong compartment," he said. "It doesn't really matter for the rest of the trip, but I wanted to ensure you know where to go in case of an emergency."

Katrina's fist tightened. "Shouldn't we get off the train if there's an emergency?"

The conductor sucked on his mustache with his bottom lip. "True enough, but not if there's a maniac on the train. Best to stay in your compartments." He winked at Tamika.

Tamika put on her best haughty professor voice. "And are we expecting a maniac to join us, Mr. Conductor?"

"You're a funny bunch, aren't you?"

Katrina rose and marched over to the conductor. Though she was the same height, her bulk was considerable next to his beanpole frame. "If there's nothing else, I'm sure you have to move on to the next compartments to harass other passengers. *Sir.*"

The conductor's cap fell off. He grabbed it and scurried away.

Zeynep and Tamika clapped.

"Bravo," said Zeynep.

Katrina took an exaggerated bow.

"Whew," said Tamika. "I was worried for a minute."

"Me too," said Zeynep as she grabbed a small carved owl out of her backpack.

"You were afraid?" asked Katrina. "But you're never afraid, Zeynep."

"Ah, but that's only because I knew what was happening over the past few weeks." She paused. "Meet Mr. Owl." She made a hoo-hoo sound and handed it to Tamika.

Tamika took Mr. Owl as if he were some unbelievable talisman. She glanced at Katrina with a worried look.

"It's such a rare side of you, Zeynep. Although I guess you did tell us you're silly."

Zeynep giggled. "Don't worry. I wanted to see how you reacted."

Tala and Adi appeared in the doorway.

"Are you alright?" asked Adi.

"We were worried," said Tala.

"We're fine. Just a conductor with a twisted sense of humor. Come in. Zeynep was about to tell us a story."

"Yes, where were we," said Tala. "Zeynep, you were about to tell us how you managed to hire a top immigration lawyer. Surely it must have drained your bank account?"

"It's not a problem. I had a few dollars to spare."

"How much, exactly?"

Zeynep glanced around shiftily and lowered her voice. "Five hundred thousand. And it's ours, all ours!"

29

───────

Katrina's jaw hung open. Had she just said five hundred thousand dollars? "Zeynep," said Katrina. "Please tell us all."

Zeynep rubbed Mr. Owl absently. "Let's see. First, before we start, you all need to understand something. If you don't, you'll be very angry with me."

"What is it?" Tala adjusted her ponytail.

"I had to lie to you all, or at least omit certain facts. Not because I wanted to, but because we couldn't take the risk that one of us would give things away." She surveyed the crowd. "Do you understand?"

Everyone nodded their head. But only slightly.

"So everything is true about the confidence trick. Except the players. I met Sidney Bickford when I first came to New York from Istanbul to pursue my master's degree. He was a business professor at the time."

"Don't tell me," breathed Tamika. "You were lovers."

Zeynep squirmed. Only Mr. Owl remained still. "Yes, sort of. For a short time, but then we became close friends. He said if I ever needed a favor, he'd be there for me."

"Impressive," said Katrina.

"When Sid moved here two years ago and set up his property business, we reconnected."

"Mmm...reconnected," said Adi with a wink.

"No. No!" Zeynep shook her head. "It wasn't like that. But I did know he had, well, a shady past. He'd been involved in all kinds of Wall Street deals which weren't exactly illegal but weren't ethical, either." She paused. "A plan formed in my mind, especially when Batu returned and I became worried about how often law enforcement was showing up on my doorstep. Sid was the only person I knew in the whole world who had power. And I mean powerful connections. I went to him about my problem. At first, I thought he would be able to send a message to local law enforcement—and even work some magic with Immigration.

"But our conversation quickly turned to Blipton. Sid was genuinely interested in higher education, and he was donating some pretty serious funds to the university. It was partly because he wanted to get on their sweet side, so his firm would have a good shot at landing property development contracts if there were any going. But it was also because he really thought it was a worthwhile cause. When I told him what I'd witnessed at Blipton, he was appalled. As appalled as all of us were, but from a different angle."

"So Sidney Bickford was in on it from the start?" said Katrina, astonished.

"Not quite from the start. At first he didn't want to get on board—it would jeopardize the position he'd spent so long building up. He was ready to back the algorithm for the deans, but only because he thought it might boost his chances of getting the contract for those new dorms. And he needed that contract—badly. It was about the only thing capable of keeping his company going. Then something happened. I think he must have read Gabriel's article in the paper. Remember the day we met him at Zephyr's?"

"And he went to Joe Aragon's," recalled Tamika. "He was so furious afterwards."

"Aragon confirmed that everything in the article was true. Sid told me afterwards that Joe's company was paying huge kickbacks to the planning department—more than he could ever afford. It would have bankrupted Bickford Inc. So he had a little, let's say, change of heart." Zeynep smiled. "He texted me and asked if he could get on board after all. That was when we had that phone call in your apartment, Adi. He knew then that whatever cash we could get out of the deans was his best option for keeping afloat.

"So together, we devised a plan for all of us to get revenge, get some money, clear out some of the bad apples in administration, and for all of us to escape."

"Mimosas!" Carlos appeared at the door with a tray full of plastic champagne glasses. The others were too stunned to react, despite his expectant air.

He approached Tala first, who smiled at him as she selected a glass.

"I can tell you all are going to be delightful passengers." He bowed, winked at Tala and withdrew.

Katrina resisted making another remark about Tala. "Continue, Zeynep."

Zeynep sipped her drink and grimaced. "Too sweet." She offered it to Katrina, who had already downed her mimosa in one gulp.

"Yes, to continue. We devised the plan which you're all familiar with. The difference was the mark wasn't going to be a trustee, and certainly wasn't going to be Sid. Though you all had to believe it to be true. No, the mark or marks were going to be the deans. They were the real problem, and we could solve all of our issues if we took them down."

"So all that nonsense about going after other trustees was a ruse?" asked Tamika.

"I'm afraid so. You all had to think Sid was the mark because otherwise your hatred of both deans would get in the way."

"Where does Sally come into this?" asked Tala.

"And what about the attempts on my life?" asked Katrina.

Zeynep held up a hand. "Let me start with the threats to Katrina and Gabriel. They were all Dean Hackett."

"How do you know?" asked Adi.

"Because it's the only logical explanation. Sid obviously wasn't involved. Bullard might have been tangentially involved, but he isn't smart enough to find his way out of a paper bag." She smiled. "Aren't you all going to congratulate me on my excellent American idiom?"

Murmurs of approval.

"So Hackett tampered with Katrina's car, sent those threatening notes, and also threatened Gabriel."

"But why?" asked Tamika.

"As Gabriel discovered, Hackett had a fanatical devotion to the university, despite his own appalling behavior. He'd go to any lengths to cover up any scandal. Remember, he had plenty of experience as he was used to covering up his own bad behavior. This time, however, he must have had a psychological breaking point which made him think it was acceptable to kill people to save the university."

Katrina nodded. "Sounds plausible, especially because he seemed increasingly unhinged. But what about Sally?"

"Ah, Sally. Sid used her, though it was easy because she was so greedy. He first met her at a donors' event where she babbled on about the trash in the neighborhood. Meaning people. Sid was so desperate to win that dorm contract, and save his company, that he dreamed up a way to skew the odds in his favor. He asked her to figure out a way to smear Aragon Partners. If the university administration thought Aragon was corrupt, they were bound to turn to Bickford, right? So she led Gabriel on about the story."

"Poor Gabriel," said Tamika. "His big scoop. And he thought Sally was thinking of the public good. I don't think I'll tell him. It was a damn good story all the same."

Zeynep nodded. "Sally told Dean Hackett about it all for good measure. I don't think she meant any harm by it, though—she couldn't have realized how unhinged he was."

"So let me get this straight." Tamika held her glass up as the train went around a sharp corner. "Sid set up Sally. Sally set up Gabriel."

"Yes. Sid played the mark to perfection. Remember the brunch?"

"Wait!" cried Katrina. "You were the one who prompted me to make noise so they'd hear us in the next booth."

Zeynep nodded. "See? There's no reason for you to feel guilty. Same thing goes with Sally breaking into Adi's apartment. Sally did so because she thought she could get Adi's information or login information since Adi has access to so many university computer systems. Sid and I had a feeling Gabriel would follow, though we weren't certain. I texted Sid that we'd be trying to get Gabriel out of the house, so he played along."

"You mean he knew we were hiding in the garage?" Tala huffed.

"Yes. Sorry. But you understand why I couldn't tell you. The whole thing had to look natural so you'd all play your parts. Which you did to perfection."

"So the whole scheme was to get the deans to buy into the scam? But Sid has the money!" Adi threw up their arms. Katrina knew it didn't take much for Adi to become tipsy.

"I had hoped for at least one dean. Two was a super bargain, especially since we wanted revenge on both of them. Sid roped them in nicely. The handoff at his place was a setup, which is exactly why I had to stop Katrina from coming to rescue Tala and Tamika too soon."

"But where did the five hundred thousand dollars come from?" asked Tala.

"Sid took the three hundred thousand dollars in cash from the deans and has escaped somewhere unknown. We, however, had the login information for the university accounts the deans gave us, remember? Well, I'm not too bad with computers. I drained one of the university accounts earmarked for the new dorms, which were really an excuse to raise rents and 'clean up the neighborhood.' So that money comes to us. And we used it to hire a lawyer."

"So you're saying the neighborhood is saved?" asked Katrina.

"Yes. I gave a generous donation to the community organizers fighting the dorms, which will hopefully stop the whole project. I doubt any construction company will touch it now."

"What about the deans? I heard they resigned," said Adi.

Katrina smiled. "I reiterated my point to Hackett about information I have about his involvement in embezzlement and a relationship with a student. He can't find me and hurt me, so he didn't have a choice."

"And as Dean Bullard's assistant," said Zeynep, "I have plenty of dirt on him involving lavish trips he took with university money. He had to resign as well. All of our resignations came in at the same time. Though we will have to figure out a way for Tala to finish her degree."

"I only have a few classes left. I'll figure it out." Tala smiled.

"What's next?" asked Adi. "Are we really going to New York?"

"I had a call from a friend at a small college in the northeast. I don't have the details yet, but she wants to hire us. That is, if you're all up for traveling away from home for a while."

Adi nodded. "I'm ready to get out—and there's really nothing keeping me here." They snorted. "Certainly no significant other."

"I'll miss Gabriel, but he'll be moving on soon anyway. He said he wants to leave town—and all my relatives are scattered, anyway," sighed Tamika.

"And Batu is my only tie to Snake's Canyon," said Zeynep. "And I'm sure he wants to leave eventually."

Katrina glanced down at her phone, half-expecting a text from Jeremy to pop up. But he still hadn't responded to the one she sent yesterday. *C'est la vie.*

She raised her glass. "Long live the pirate queens!"

The End

Did you enjoy this book? If so, I'd appreciate a thoughtful review on Amazon. Thank you!

ENJOYED THE PIRATE QUEENS?

I rely on you, dear reader, to help me spread the word about this series. A thoughtful review on Amazon will help other readers find the book. Thank you!

If you'd like discounts and updates on new releases, you can join my reader group here.

The next book in the series, *The Warden's Cove Caper*, will be released soon!

rl@rldonovanauthor.com

ABOUT THE AUTHOR

RL Donovan loves mysteries, thrillers, capers, and puzzles—anything with a twist. As a former academic, RL uses the unbelievable but true escapades of her colleagues and students to create absurd scenarios for her books.

rl@rldonovanauthor.com